# EXPECTING FORTUNE'S HEIR

*CINDY KIRK*

HARLEQUIN® SPECIAL EDITION®

Special thanks and acknowledgment to Cindy Kirk
for her contribution to
The Fortunes of Texas: Southern Invasion continuity.

Recycling programs
for this product may
not exist in your area.

ISBN-13: 978-0-373-65740-7

EXPECTING FORTUNE'S HEIR

HARLEQUIN®
www.Harlequin.com

**Printed in U.S.A.**

### *"I have something I've wanted to tell you, too,"* Lia said.

Shane smiled. "Anyone ever tell you that you're cute when you're serious?"

A warmth crept up Lia's neck. She moistened her dry lips with the tip of her tongue.

Heat flared in his eyes.

"This is important."

The slight tremor in her voice brought a slight frown of concern to his forehead.

"No worries." The gentle kindness in his tone was nearly her undoing. "You can tell me anything."

Before Lia could get a single word past her suddenly stiff lips, his phone buzzed. He grimaced. "I'm sorry but I need to take this. It shouldn't take long."

Lia exhaled the breath she didn't realize she'd been holding. Perhaps she should be grateful she'd been granted a slight reprieve. The only problem was, it was temporary. Because the news that she had for Shane was something he needed to hear. And he needed to hear it tonight.

Dear Reader,

Because I'm a big fan of the Fortune family, I was thrilled when asked to write this book. I've always found each member of this wealthy yet cohesive group intriguing. Writing Shane and Lia's story was a labor of love. It allowed me to not only bring Shane to life, but other members of his family as well.

I came from a small family and always wished I had a boatload of brothers and sisters. And, since I'm being honest, I wished my family had a lot of money, too. Perhaps that's why I love the Fortunes. They have it all. In addition, they are each getting the love of their life. Who could ask for more?

Warmest regards,

Cindy Kirk

## Books by Cindy Kirk

Harlequin Special Edition

Silhouette Special Edition

Harlequin Books

\*Meet Me in Montana
†Rx for Love
\*\*The Fortunes of Texas: Southern Invasion

Other titles by this author available in ebook format.

---

## *CINDY KIRK*

has loved to read for as long as she can remember. In first grade she received an award for reading one hundred books. As she grew up, summers were her favorite time of year. Nothing beat going to the library, then coming home and curling up in front of the window air conditioner with a good book. Often the novels she read would spur ideas, and she'd make up her own story (always with a happy ending). When she'd go to bed at night, instead of counting sheep, she'd make up more stories in her head. Since selling her first story to Harlequin Books in 1999, Cindy has been forced to juggle her love of reading with her passion for creating stories of her own…but she doesn't mind. Writing for the Harlequin Special Edition series is a dream come true. She only hopes you have as much fun reading her books as she has writing them!

Cindy invites you to visit her website, www.cindykirk.com.

To my wonderful friend Susan Powers Alexander.

## *Chapter One*

*New Year's Eve*

His eyes were the bluest Natalia Serrano had ever seen.

Of course, she was a fair distance away and it could have been just a trick of the light. Still, he was a magnificent specimen in his black tux; tall with a lean, muscular build and a classically handsome face. A lock of dark hair tumbled to his forehead and he impatiently pushed it back.

He was older than her twenty-five years—she'd guess early thirties. His self-assured and confident stance told her he was used to giving orders, not taking them.

Although she would guess they had little in common, in that moment she knew there was one thing they did share... and that was loneliness. Their gazes met, and her lips lifted in a tentative smile. The connection she felt was so strong that she expected him to cross the room and say hello, or at least return her smile. Instead he frowned, turned and disappeared into the hallway.

A loud cheer rose from the crowd and Natalia returned her attention to the revelers on the dance club floor, all ready to usher in a new year with kisses, hugs and a champagne toast. They looked so happy, so in the moment.

The band, a popular one from nearby San Antonio, had quickly gotten the crowd pumped up and now kept them at a fevered pitch. The waitstaff, easily identifiable by their black pants and cream-colored Western shirts with black longhorns monogrammed above the hotel moniker, kept the alcohol flowing.

La Casa Paloma, an elegant hotel in downtown Red Rock, Texas, had gone all out to make this a New Year's Eve to remember. Linen-clad tables, complete with noise-makers and party hats, formed a U shape around a large dance floor. The entire ballroom ceiling was covered with a glittery silver netting. Captured in it were hundreds of balloons, which would be released at midnight.

*Midnight.* Natalia glanced at her watch face surrounded by multicolored glass beads and emitted a groan. Still ninety minutes to go.

Across the mass of gyrating bodies she saw her best friend pressed up against a guy Natalia didn't recognize. Though she and Selina had come together, there was no expectation they'd leave together. Which was good considering Natalia was ready to call it an evening. For Selina the night appeared to be just getting started.

"Hey, beautiful. Want to dance?"

Natalia turned and gazed into the blurry eyes of a cowboy who'd already had too much to drink. His baby face and youthful features reminded her of her brother Eric around the time he'd turned twenty-one and had been into hell-raising.

"I'm sorry." She softened the refusal with a smile. "I'm here with someone."

Until recently that would have been the truth. She and David Francisco had been together for almost a year. But a couple months ago, whatever fabric had held them together had begun to unravel. Last month they'd split for good.

The cowboy blinked and looked first to her left and then to her right. Confusion blanketed his face. "I don't see anyone."

"He's in the restroom."

"Oh." The cowboy's lips hitched up in a crooked grin even as he listed slightly to the left. "I'm headed there now myself. I'll tell him where you are."

Natalia hid a smile. Since she hadn't described who she was supposedly with, that might prove a bit difficult but she appreciated the offer. "Thanks."

When he disappeared into the crowd, she stepped out the closest door into the large, well-manicured courtyard that ran the entire length of the rear of the hotel.

The gray-haired guard looked up from where he was seated. "You'll need your hand stamped if you plan to go back inside."

"Not necessary." Natalia shook her head, sending long black hair cascading down her back. "I'm headed home."

Surprise lit the older man's eyes. "You're not staying for the balloon drop?"

"I'm afraid not." She gently tapped one temple. "I'm getting a headache."

It wasn't a lie. Natalia had been fighting a sinus infection for over a week. Once she'd started on an antibiotic, she'd felt a thousand times better. Still, the loud music and the potent perfume in the air *had* brought a twinge of pain back.

"Well, I hope you feel better soon." He patted her on the shoulder. "Happy New Year."

The kindness in his voice was nearly her undoing. Natalia had never known her father. He'd left when she was small.

"Thank you." Impulsively she gave him a hug. "Happy New Year to you, too."

Redness traveled up his neck.

"If you change your mind, come back," he sputtered as the blush reached his weathered face. "I'll let you in."

Natalia returned his smile and gave a wave before sauntering off. Since she didn't have anywhere to go—except home to an empty apartment—she took time to enjoy the beauty of the deserted courtyard festooned with white lights.

She wandered down the flagstone walkway, admiring the shiny green foliage lining the path. When she reached the elaborate decorative gate that led to the street, Natalia returned to a wrought iron bench she'd passed moments before and took a seat.

The Manolo Blahnik slingbacks she'd picked up at a consignment store in San Antonio were superstylish but a half size too small. Natalia knew she was playing with fire when she unhooked each buckle and slipped them off. Getting them back on might not be all that easy.

But as her fingers massaged her instep, she decided it was worth the risk. For the first time all evening she found herself relaxing. The band sounded better from a distance and she could once again feel her toes.

Life would be practically perfect if she'd thought to bring a wrap. Though the temperature was in the upper forties—which was nice for a late-December evening—her one-shouldered minidress in a thin jersey fabric wasn't nearly warm enough.

Natalia hugged her arms around herself, not yet ready to head to the front of the hotel to catch a cab. Though her early departure from the party might not show it, Natalia loved this time of year. Loved the hope of a new beginning. Loved the promise of a new year stretched out before her.

Footsteps sounded on the flagstone and Natalia looked up just in time to see the handsome stranger from the party round the corner of a tall sculptured bush. For one crazy second she thought he'd come looking for her, until she saw the surprise on his face.

It was a silly thought anyway. They'd never spoken or even been introduced. Though she swore their eyes had met and connected, for all Natalia knew he could have been looking at one of the other women around her.

"I didn't realize anyone else was out here." His voice was deep, with a hint of a Southern accent.

"If you were headed to this bench—" despite a thousand hummingbird wings fluttering in her chest, Natalia's voice came out cool and offhand "—there's plenty of room. Anyway, I was just about to leave."

"Don't rush off on my account." He sat beside her, leaving a respectable distance between them. "Besides, it's not midnight. Who leaves a New Year's Eve party before midnight?"

"Well, I did. And it looks like you did." She smiled. "That makes two of us."

He didn't comment on her observation. Instead his gaze had dropped to her bare feet and to the shoes sitting in front of her.

Natalia resisted the urge to wiggle her toes and to ask him what he thought about her deep purple toenail polish. Personally she thought it went perfectly with her orchid-colored minidress.

"Shoes hurting your feet?"

Natalia sighed. "They're half a size too small."

A look of puzzlement crossed his face. "Why did you buy them?"

"They were a bargain." She stopped short of telling him she'd gotten them secondhand. The cut of his tux was too perfect to be a rental. That told her this was a man who'd probably never set foot into a thrift store or consignment shop in his life. He'd never understand the thrill of getting for two hundred dollars a pair of shoes that retailed for eight hundred dollars.

"They're Manolos."

An amused smile lifted his lips. "That explains it."

"I bet most of the women were wearing these at your bash."

His expression stilled. A shutter dropped over his eyes. "My bash?"

Natalia rolled her eyes, not bothering to hide her reaction to his ridiculous response. "You're wearing a tux," she pointed out. "Way too fancy for the party inside."

The corners of his eyes crinkled, softening the hard planes of his elegant features. "You don't like the way I'm dressed?"

"I never said that." Natalia responded to his teasing tone with a lighthearted lilt. "But you don't fit in. So, where did you come from?"

"Georgia," he said with a disarming smile.

"That's not what I meant."

He lifted a shoulder in a slight shrug. "Is it important?"

Natalia resisted the urge to sigh, suddenly weary of the game. She grabbed her shoes and stood. "I need to go."

"Please stay." Those incredible blue eyes met hers and she found it hard to deny him anything.

Or maybe it wasn't the eyes but the expensive cologne that teased her nostrils. It wasn't the department store Polo that David had worn or any of her brothers' favorites. It was a scent she couldn't identify, but found extremely enticing.

He guided her back into her seat.

"You smell good," she said, not feeling the need to play games.

"Thank you." His lips twitched. "So do you."

Natalia sighed. "Go ahead."

"Go ahead...what?"

"Tell me I smell like your mother."

Confusion contorted his face. "Why would I say that?"

"It's Chanel. Every guy I've dated has had a mother or a grandmother who wears this scent." She lifted her chin. "I don't care. I like it."

"Well, just to be clear, I like it, too. And neither my mother nor my grandmothers have ever smelled as good as you."

"Oh."

"They've also never looked as good as you, either." He reached over and before she could stop him, his hand slid up her thigh, his fingers slipping just inside the bottom hem of her dress.

A feeling of heat shot up her thigh to pool between her legs. She slapped his hand. "What are you doing?"

"It looked...stretchy," he said, the top of his ears turning red. "I thought I'd check it out."

"How would you like it if I slid my hand inside your pants?"

The minute the words left Natalia's mouth she realized they'd come out all wrong.

Unexpectedly he grinned. "I'd like it just fine. Go ahead."

She shook her head. Between the intoxicating scent of his cologne and the testosterone rolling off him in waves, Natalia felt a bit tipsy. But not drunk enough to act on her outrageous comment.

Still, she couldn't help wondering what she'd find there.

She knew it wasn't size that mattered, but what a man could do with it—how he treated a woman. Unfortunately, David cared more for his own pleasure than hers.

Would this guy be like David? Or would he—

She stopped the speculation before it could fully form. In his parting remarks, David had told her she was a cold fish and that was why he had to look elsewhere. But right now she didn't feel cold; she felt…hot. Just thinking of this man touching her, really, truly touching her, made her shiver with desire.

"You're cold." Before Natalia realized what was happening, Mr. Blue Eyes removed his jacket and settled it around her shoulders.

The garment retained the heat of his body and that wonderful delicious smell. She snuggled into it, suddenly feeling very warm indeed.

"If I'm going to wear your jacket, I should at least know your name," she said in a light, teasing tone.

"Shane."

So it was to be first names only. That suited her just fine. They could talk, perhaps flirt a little then go their separate ways.

"I'm Lia." Though Natalia was what everyone knew her by, Lia was what her family called her.

"Le-ah," he said in a husky voice that made her blood feel like warm honey sliding through her veins. "A beautiful name for a beautiful woman."

She gazed up at him through lowered lashes, not able to hide her smile. "Does that line really work for you?"

"Sometimes." Shane chuckled, a low, pleasant rumbling sound. "But you are beautiful. The moonlight shimmers in your dark hair like diamonds on silk."

He lightly touched one long curl. When she didn't pull

away, he let his hand linger, his fingers sliding deeper. "Soft, too."

His gaze dropped to her lips. When he looked up, she knew what he wanted.

A kiss. No big deal. It was New Year's Eve. Lots of people kissed strangers when the clock struck twelve. Of course, it wasn't yet midnight but she wasn't going to quibble over an hour.

"Do you believe in love?"

Lia reined in her lascivious thoughts and met his gaze. "I love my mother. And my brother."

"I'm not talking about that kind of love," he said in a voice that reminded her of smooth, rich bourbon. "I'm talking about true love. The love between a man and a woman."

Lia stiffened, for a second worried he was about to give her that "love at first sight" line. She'd fallen for it once. She wouldn't be that stupid again. But when she looked in his eyes, there was no I-fell-for-you-the-second-I-saw-you nonsense that David had laid on her, which she'd naively taken as gospel.

"I'd like to believe it exists, but I'm not so sure it does," she said honestly.

"It doesn't," he said and a shutter dropped over his eyes. "I used to believe it did, but not anymore."

She surreptitiously glanced at his ring finger. Of course, some men didn't wear a ring. "Are you married? Do you have a girlfriend?"

"No to both questions." He frowned. "If I had a wife or a girlfriend, I wouldn't be here talking with you."

"Ever been married?"

He made a sound of irritation low in his throat and shook his head.

"Ever come close?"

"Not really." His gaze turned sharp and assessing. "What about you?"

"No husband. No boyfriend." Lia kept her tone calm and matter-of-fact. "As far as coming close…"

She remembered David and all his plans for "their" future. Now she realized their relationship had been simply a house of cards. He'd spun his lies. She'd become suspicious but hadn't trusted her gut.

"My boyfriend and I recently broke up," she said finally. "How can you love someone you can't trust? You know what I mean?"

He nodded, his lips pulled together in a grim semblance of a smile. "You're preaching to the choir on that one, darlin'."

So she wasn't the only one who'd been dumped on. Though it made no sense, somehow it made her feel better. Impulsively she reached over and took his hand. "We don't need liars and cheats," she said fervently. "All we need is ourselves."

"Amen." He lifted her hand to his mouth and pressed a kiss into her palm.

A smoldering heat flared through her, a sensation she didn't bother to fight.

"But sometimes it's nice to hold someone close. To feel their skin against yours. To simply go with the moment." His voice had become a husky caress. And his eyes—she'd never seen such beautiful blue eyes. Eyes that tempted her to venture from the firm shore of what she'd always known to a place where she could be over her head in seconds. "Interested?"

Time seemed to stretch and extend.

After a moment, Lia cocked her head. "Are you asking if I'd be interested in a one-night stand?"

"Darn if you aren't a direct one." The tiny lines around

his eyes crinkled when he laughed, making him look boy-ish and years younger. "Yeah, that's exactly what I'm ask-ing."

*Just say no,* the tiny voice in her head that was her moral compass cried out. *Get up and walk away.*

Lia hadn't had many lovers—David was her second—and she'd never made love outside of a committed rela-tionship. Never considered making love with a stranger.

Until tonight.

"Do you have condoms?" she asked, as if she was ac-tually considering his offer. Which she wasn't. Not at all.

"I always holster my gun."

She took that to be a yes. But what did it matter? She certainly wasn't going to sleep with a stranger, no matter how sexy he was, or how hot and bothered he made her feel. Her mother had taught her that sex belonged within the bonds of a relationship with a man she loved. Not with a blue-eyed stranger.

"Shane." Lia paused, not sure what she wanted to say.

"Perhaps this will help you decide." The words had barely left his lips when he pulled her to him.

As if in a dream, she wound her arms around his neck and lifted her face.

He folded her more fully into his arms, anchoring her against his chest as his mouth covered hers in a deep, com-pelling kiss. Lia stroked his thick hair. He tasted as sweet as spearmint candy.

His hand closed over one breast, circling the peak with his fingers. Lia inhaled sharply and for a second, panicked. Until she remembered this was simply a brief interlude, not a prelude to sex.

If he'd noticed her momentary hesitation he gave no in-dication. He continued to kiss her with a slow thorough-ness that left her weak, trembling and longing for more.

"Come with me to my suite," he murmured.

She planted a kiss at the base of his neck, his skin salty beneath her lips.

"Are you sure that would be wise?" Her words seemed to come from far away.

"No." He leaned toward her and whispered in her ear, "But let's do it anyway."

## Chapter Two

On the way to the top floor of the hotel, Lia realized she'd let her desire for this blue-eyed stranger cloud her judgment. She couldn't sleep with this man. No matter how much she liked holding hands with him and listening to his Southern drawl. No matter how much she liked the way he gently teased her about the size-too-small shoes dangling from his fingers. When he slipped his key card out of his pocket, she decided it was time to confess she'd made a mistake. Lia gently lifted her shoes from his hand and offered him a bright smile. "Thanks for carrying these for me."

Shane turned and Lia could see the wheels turning in his head. A smart man, he missed very little. But he obviously hadn't seen this coming. "You're leaving?"

The disbelieving look on his face told her this was not a man accustomed to having his invitations declined.

"I'm afraid so." She took a step back, real regret in her

tone. "This kind of thing, well, it's not me. It's not who I am. I don't hop into bed with someone I just met."

His gaze scanned her face, his eyes clear and very blue. A rueful smile tipped his lips. "Truth is, it's not something I usually do, either."

"But *you'd* have gone through with it."

He shrugged even as his smile began to widen.

"C'mon, fess up," she teased.

She didn't know why she bothered. The heat simmering in his electric blue eyes gave the answer.

"You're very beautiful, Lia." His eyes grew dark and she saw a flash of pain before a shutter dropped over them. "And I don't want to be alone tonight."

Telling her she was beautiful was simply what men said to get a woman into bed. But it was the part about not wanting to be alone that made her realize her first impression had been correct.

Despite his obvious intelligence, charm and money, whatever was going on in Shane's life had left him not only alone—but lonely—on New Year's Eve.

Lia could definitely empathize. "I—"

"Look." The set of his face turned austere, rigid, as if carved in granite. "If you want to stay, stay. If you don't…"

He left the rest unsaid, leaving the choice up to her. Despite the fact they were almost strangers, knowing he was also lonely made her feel close to him. She glanced at her watch. Thirty minutes until midnight. "How about I come in, we have a drink and talk?"

The moment the words left her mouth, Lia resisted the urge to groan. Shane hadn't invited her up to his suite for her conversational skills. She'd been invited up for one specific purpose and now she was changing the rules.

"Forget it," Lia said before he'd had a chance to respond.

"I'm sure you don't want to spend what's left of the evening *talking* with me. I'll just—"

"Stay. I want you to stay." His hand closed over hers and she felt a jolt of electricity. "There's champagne in the room. And I had the refrigerator stocked with some of my favorite foods. Or I can order whatever you like."

Lia took a steadying breath and considered her options. Go home and ring in the New Year alone. Or stay and get to know Shane better. "I love champagne. But I'm warning you, no funny business."

His head cocked to one side. "Would that be the same as monkey business?"

"Shane—" she began then stopped when she saw his lips twitch.

He pushed open the door and stepped aside to let her enter first. "Does a kiss at midnight fall under funny or monkey business?"

Lia had already experienced one kiss from this man. She wasn't sure her resolve to keep her distance could withstand another one. "It falls under both."

He chuckled. "Somehow I thought that's what you'd say."

Shane ushered her through the entryway into a parlor larger than her entire apartment. The placard outside the door had informed her this was the Lone Star Suite.

The name fit the decor. The transom above the double balcony doors had a leaded glass window with a hand-painted, kiln-fired rendering of a cattle drive. A custom knotty-pine fireplace filled one wall; a large flat-screen television was mounted over the mantel. A caramel-colored leather sofa with matching chair and ottoman were positioned comfortably near the fireplace. Several table lamps gave the room a golden glow.

"It's lovely," she managed to say when she found her voice.

Shane dropped the key card on a side table. "Would you like the grand tour?"

There was a spark of mischief in his eyes that she found disconcerting.

"No, but if you could point me in the direction of the bathroom, I'd appreciate it."

He grinned and gestured toward a long hallway. "I'll have the champagne poured and ready by the time you return."

Lia dropped her shoes by the sofa and scampered down the hall in her bare feet. She was already past the bedroom when she realized the door was open. Slowing her steps, she turned back, unable to resist taking a quick peek inside.

The hunter-green bedcovers on the massive king-size bed had been turned back, revealing cream-colored sheets that looked soft and inviting. There was also a desk, a large dresser and, of course, another television. But her eyes kept returning to the bed.

Was this where they would have made love—er, had sex? Though she was twenty-five, Lia had only been physically intimate with her college boyfriend—who had been just as inexperienced as her—and then there had been David.

David was the one who'd made her realize she didn't have a particularly strong sex drive. In fact, she suspected her inability to please him was part of the reason he'd looked elsewhere.

Just thinking about taking her clothes off and hopping into bed with Shane both thrilled and terrified her. She'd probably be a big disappointment to him, too. Lia sighed and pulled her gaze away from the bed.

*The bathroom,* she told herself. *Find the bathroom.*

She couldn't wait to see how that room measured up to the high standards set by the rest of the suite. The second she stepped inside, the sight of the ten-foot Texas Lone Star stained-glass window above the whirlpool tub stole her breath away. By the time she caught a glimpse of the rain showerhead hanging from the ceiling, she realized every inch of this luxurious suite was first-class. Anyone who could afford to stay here was way out of her league.

Her small apartment, next to the Red Rock Medical Clinic, was in the poorer part of town. There were no mechanical rain showers or soaking tubs in her bathroom. No ten-foot stained-glass windows. Heck, the bed in her apartment came out of the wall and the kitchen had less counter space than this bathroom.

After splashing some cold water on her face, Lia padded back down the hallway, *goodbye* already poised on her lips. After getting a glimpse into Shane's world, she realized how different her life was from his. What could she have to say that could possibly interest him?

When she reached the parlor, she noticed a fire now burned cheerily in the hearth. A tray of appetizers sat on a glossy pine coffee table. Shane moved forward to greet her with a chilled glass of champagne. His tie hung loose around his neck and the top button of his shirt was undone.

He looked much more approachable and relaxed than he had when she'd left him. It was as if he was actually looking forward to their conversation…unless that was simply her own wishful thinking.

Since he'd gone to so much effort, Lia decided it wouldn't hurt to stay for a *few* minutes. She took a sip of the champagne, the vintage dry and sparkling crisp on her tongue. "This is wonderful."

He shot her a wink. "I aim to please."

*Such a charmer.* She took a seat at one end of the sofa, careful not to spill the drink in her hand.

"Where are you from, Shane?" she asked again, hoping he'd be straight with her.

"Atlanta." He sat beside her, once again leaving some distance between them.

Lia felt oddly disappointed, but reminded herself it wasn't as if she *wanted* him to sit close. Or did she?

"I noticed your watch, earlier." Shane relaxed back against the leather cushion, an easy smile on his lips. "Very nice. Unique. I'm not sure I've seen one like that before."

The beadwork was her own design, the colors and style chosen specifically to complement her dress tonight. "I made it."

"Pardon?"

"Not the watch," she clarified, taking another sip of champagne. "The band. I designed it and did the beading. That's what I do. I'm an artist. Beadwork is my medium."

His gaze returned to her wrist and warmth traveled up her arm. He lifted his glass, but paused before drinking. "I don't think I know anyone who does beading."

Of course he didn't. The kind of people he hung out with were probably CEOs and successful business owners. Titans of industry. The kind of men and women who belonged to the exclusive Red Rock Country Club, located on the edge of town.

"Eventually I hope to do it full-time," she told him. "For now, I fit it in as I can."

While she didn't love her job as an accountant at a small manufacturing firm, she liked the regular paycheck. Unfortunately, there had recently been rumors about possible cutbacks after the first of the year.

"You're a creative person." He suddenly smiled, as if the sun had broken through the clouds. "I'm impressed."

A warm fuzzy glow that had nothing to do with the alcohol she'd consumed washed over Lia. They talked for several minutes about her design process and how a vision for a piece came together.

"You said you'd like to do it full-time." His gaze didn't stray from her face. "Have you developed a business plan?"

Before she could answer, he tossed a few other questions into the mix. Thanks to her various business and entrepreneurial projects in college, Lia not only understood what he was asking, she could intelligently respond. As the conversation continued, she felt the last of her tension melt away.

"Tell me about the boyfriend who burned you," he asked after she finished describing the intricate beaded necklace she'd recently designed around an oval porcelain cameo.

Lia blinked. "Did I say he burned me?"

Shane took a sip of champagne, his gaze never leaving her face. "You said you couldn't trust him."

At the moment she was having difficulty recalling exactly what she'd said about David. She tilted her glass of champagne and realized it was empty. "Do you have more of this?"

Shane lifted the bottle from the granite-topped coffee table and filled her crystal flute. "The boyfriend?" he prompted.

Lia briefly considered telling him her and David's breakup was none of his concern. Not because she wanted to protect her ex-boyfriend, but because she was ashamed of being so, well, gullible.

*There's no shame in trusting someone.* That was what her mother had told her when Lia had called and said she'd broken it off with David and why.

"I discovered he'd been cheating on me." She kept her tone matter-of-fact. "Apparently the reason he hadn't been around much was because he'd been spending most of his free time in San Antonio with his new girlfriend."

He gave her an imperceptible nod. "You didn't suspect?"

Lia glanced sharply at him. But there was no judgment in his eyes. Only curiosity.

"After about a month of excuses and stories that didn't make sense, I confronted him." She rubbed the bridge of her nose to forestall a sudden headache. Sweet Lord, how she hated to tell this story. "He told me his mother—her name is Rose—had been diagnosed with end-stage cancer and he'd been spending the time with her. She was a widow, living in San Antonio. I'd met her several times and liked her."

Shane leaned forward, his brows pulled together.

"Of course, I wanted to call right away and set up a time to see her. But David insisted his mom didn't want to talk with anyone but family. I later found out Rose doesn't have cancer, never had cancer. She wasn't dying. She—"

Her voice cracked. She'd been so worried about his mother and then to realize it had all been a lie...

She clamped her mouth shut and drew in a ragged breath.

Shane's jaw set at a hard angle. "He was living a double life."

Lia nodded. "I don't understand why he didn't simply tell me the truth."

"It's hard when a person's actions don't make sense." He shifted his gaze to the fire for several heartbeats. "And damn frustrating when they lie to you."

Unexpectedly Shane reached over and gave her hand a squeeze. And instead of immediately pulling away, she let his hand linger.

"I'm over it now," she told him just as her phone began to play a tinny version of "Auld Lang Syne."

He lifted a brow.

Lia scrambled to her feet. It didn't feel right to welcome in the New Year seated on a sofa. "I set my alarm for midnight."

"So the New Year has arrived." He rose to his feet to stand beside her just as the clock on the mantel began to chime, deep and low.

She smiled. "According to my iPhone and your clock."

He lifted his glass and tapped it against hers. "Happy New Year, Lia."

"Happy New Year, Shane."

Through the closed windows she heard fireworks exploding outside. Lia put down her glass and stepped out onto the balcony overlooking Main Street. The sky was awash in bursts of red, silvery-white and blue as well as vibrant greens and yellows.

Shane moved to stand behind her. She jumped a little as he rested his hand on her shoulder, but there was nothing suggestive in his touch. He just stood there, smelling terrific and watching the fireworks with her.

"This is much nicer than a crowded ballroom with a bunch of drunk cowboys trying to kiss me," she murmured, her gaze focused on the raucous crowd below.

"Well, I'm not drunk. And I'm not a cowboy." Shane turned her in his arms to face him. His fingers were not quite steady as they touched the curve of her cheek and trailed along the line of her jaw. "But I'd sure like to kiss you."

His seductively soft voice sent shivers rippling across her skin.

Lia cleared her suddenly dry throat. "Kissing at midnight is practically a New Year's Eve tradition."

It was all the encouragement he needed. Shane's mouth brushed slowly over hers.

When she made no effort to pull away, he settled her closely to him, as his tongue teased the fullness of her lower lip. She opened her mouth and he changed the angle of the kiss and deepened it.

Her hands moved up and she curled her fingers into the fabric of his shirt. She could feel the heat of his body under her hands, the steady thud of his heart.

Everything faded except the need to feel more of him, taste more of him.

His hands dipped down to the small of her back and pulled her closer. His erection pressed against her belly, inspiring a dizzying myriad of sensual images of her and him, in that big king-size bed, together.

But when his fingers began to tug at her zipper, Lia forced herself to pull back.

"That was nice," she managed to stammer, her breath coming in short puffs.

"Nice?" Shane looked comically appalled.

If Lia had been unprepared for the alarming rush of pleasure from his kiss, she was even less prepared to quantify the experience. "I—I should leave."

"What's the rush? Stay and help me eat these." He gave her an encouraging smile and gestured to the appetizers. "Have another glass of champagne."

Lia thought for a moment. She could fight the loud, boisterous—and likely drunk—crowds that would have filled the streets to watch the fireworks. Or she could have another glass of champagne with Shane, enjoy some sushi *then* head home. "Okay, but no more kissing."

Shane looked at her steadily. The air crackled with electricity, while one corner of his mouth curled upward. "If that's what you want."

Of course that wasn't what she *wanted*. But one of them had to be sensible. "That's what I want."

Over a couple spring rolls and some yellowfin that had to have been a special request of his, they talked. Or rather, he asked questions and she talked. About being raised by a single mother and growing up with an overprotective older brother. She told him how she'd wanted a fine arts degree but that her oldest brother, Eric, had pushed her to get a degree in business.

Shane drank some champagne and leaned back, watching her speculatively. "You can't go wrong with a degree in business."

Lia rolled her eyes. "Now you sound like my brother."

"I don't feel like your brother," he said with disarming frankness. His gaze flickered downward and lingered on her mouth for several seconds.

The brief glance touched Lia like a heated caress, sending her pulse into double time.

"Stay with me tonight." Shane touched a single fingertip to her bare shoulder then slowly dragged it down her arm. Goose bumps beaded her flesh, completely at odds with the inferno his feather-soft touch ignited.

"You are so sexy." He tucked a strand of hair behind her ear, his gaze dark and intense. "So incredibly lovely."

Unexpected desire, hot and insistent, gushed through her, turning her limp. She'd thought she was incapable of wanting a man in this way. But right now she wanted Shane.

It wasn't as if they were strangers, Lia told herself. Shane knew more about her family and her dreams for the future than a lot of her friends.

Neither of them was looking for a relationship. She wasn't ready for another one. And he, well, he seemed to have his reasons.

Though she'd always believed sex belonged in a committed relationship, she'd dated David for over a year and look how that had turned out.

Lia's gaze lingered on the man sitting beside her, patiently waiting for her answer. She searched his eyes and saw desire, hot and liquid, but also a heart-tugging uncertainty.

Her gaze flickered down to where his thumb drew a slow circle on her palm.

She and Shane were two mature adults who would be going into tonight with their eyes wide open.

She was on the pill.

He had condoms.

What could go wrong?

The next morning, Lia opened her eyes to the sound of voices. Or rather, a single voice. Shane's voice.

Pushing aside the covers, she sat up and realized she was naked. The events of the previous evening flooded back in brilliant color. They hadn't just done it once; they'd made love for hours.

A blush stole up her neck. Shane was an imaginative and inventive lover who'd seemed as interested in her pleasure as in his. When she'd warned him she was bad in bed, he'd simply laughed and went about proving her wrong.

She heard his voice again and realized he was on the phone. This gave her the perfect opportunity to hop into the shower and get dressed. Grabbing her underwear and clothes from the floor, she scampered into the bathroom and locked the door.

When she emerged fully dressed fifteen minutes later, Shane was sitting on the bed. Instead of the tux, he wore black pants and a white cotton shirt. He must have gotten up early because she could see that he'd already shaved and showered.

"I hope I didn't wake you."

Lia lifted a brow.

"I was on the phone and things got a little loud."

"Is something wrong?"

"Nothing that I can't handle," he said with a smile that didn't reach his eyes.

Lia had been around enough to know when someone was telling her to mind her own business. No matter how it had seemed last night, just because she and Shane had shared a bottle of champagne and slept together didn't make them friends.

She experienced a sudden urge to cry. How could she have had sex with him? Dear God, she didn't even know his last name. And to ask now would make it appear she was hoping for something more from him. Unless he wanted more...

"I'd better get moving." She waved a careless hand in the air. "I have things to do, places to go."

His gaze turned speculative as he leaned against the headboard. She had the sinking feeling he could see right into her head.

"It, well, it was fun." She cringed as the words came out of her mouth. *Fun?* Throwing a ball to a dog was fun. Having sex with a stranger, well, that fell more into the *crazy* range.

She started past him, hoping to find her purse in the parlor. But he grabbed her hand and tugged her to him.

"I like you, Lia," he said, his eyes dark and very blue. "But—"

Lia had no trouble filling in the blank when he paused. *I like you but this was a one-night thing. I like you but I lied—I really do have a girlfriend. I like you but—*

"I'm leaving Red Rock today," he said. "I'm not sure when I'll be back."

"Well, then, safe travels to wherever you're headed," she heard herself say, pleased at how composed she sounded. "It was a pleasure meeting you."

A slow smile spread across his face. "No kiss goodbye?"

He obviously found this situation amusing, rather than awkward. Well, good for him. For her part, she wasn't going to compound her error in judgment by delaying her departure one more second.

"I think there's been enough kissing," Lia said drily. "Have a nice life, Shane."

She turned on her heel and walked out of the suite. A woman knew when a guy was giving her the brush-off. When that happened, the only thing she had left was her dignity.

Lia didn't look back or slow down. Not even when she thought she heard him call her name.

## Chapter Three

On a bright sunny day in late April, Lia pulled her car to a stop next to the curb in front of a nightclub being built on the edge of Red Rock. Construction workers in faded blue jeans, white T-shirts and yellow hard hats were congregated under a large shade tree eating their lunch.

With the air conditioner running, Lia rolled down the passenger-side window and took a moment to survey the site. Dismay clogged her throat. From the way her brother Eric had talked when they'd spoken on the phone, Miguel Mendoza's nightclub was ready to open. Which meant his friend might be in the market for an accountant.

Though the doors and windows had been installed, the siding had yet to be put on the building. Mounds of dirt littered with construction debris filled the yard.

Heaving a resigned sigh, Lia rolled up the window then stepped out of her car. It had been two months since she'd lost her job. Savings from her beadwork sales had kept a roof over her head and food on the table since the regular paychecks had stopped. But that money was running out.

She gazed down at her loose-fitting blousy dress, confident that no one would ever suspect she was pregnant. She had the feeling Miguel would be hesitant to hire her if he knew she was expecting.

After all, his new nightclub would be going full steam by the time she gave birth in the fall. While Miguel might have his doubts, Lia knew she could handle work and motherhood. She had no choice. She would be the sole support of her child.

This certainly wasn't the life she'd once envisioned for herself and her future children. While her childhood home had been filled with lots of love, she'd witnessed firsthand the challenges her mother faced as a single parent. That was why Lia had been determined that any children she would have would grow up in a home with two loving parents.

Lia thought back to New Year's Eve and her encounter with Shane. Recalled how she'd convinced herself nothing could go wrong. She couldn't believe she'd been so reckless. No, she corrected herself almost immediately, not reckless. She'd been on the pill. They had used condoms each time. But she'd also been on antibiotics for a sinus infection, which decreased the pill's effectiveness. And, as she'd so recently discovered, no birth control method was 100 percent effective.

She'd finally told her mother the news over the phone last week. In a way, not being able to afford to fly to Boston and tell her in person had been a blessing.

Though over a thousand miles separated them, Lia had heard the disappointment in her mother's voice. At first her mom had assumed it was David's baby. But Lia had to tell her that no, she hadn't been with David in that way for months before this happened.

That had been the easy part. Telling her devoutly religious mother that she'd had a one-night stand with a man she'd never met before, a man she had no way of contacting, had been brutal. The stunned silence on the other end of the line had been worse than any words of reproach her mother could have uttered.

Yet, after she'd recovered from the initial shock, her mother had pledged her support. She'd even urged Lia to come live with her.

But Red Rock was home. Lia had been born here, grown up here. That was why two years ago when her mother had moved to Boston, Lia had remained in Texas.

Even if Lia hadn't valued her independence, her mother had enough on her plate caring for her own aging parents. Besides, if Lia gave up now, what kind of example would she be setting for her child? That when life got tough you quit and ran home to Mommy? No, she had to do better—she *would do better.*

Unfortunately, staying in Red Rock meant she was essentially in this alone. Without knowing Shane's last name, there was little chance of her ever finding him.

"It will be okay," Lia murmured under her breath. "I'll love you enough for two, *mi amorcito.*"

The words had barely left her lips when, out of the corner of her eye, Lia saw a shiny black pickup pull to a stop at the corner light. The dark-haired passenger was too busy speaking with the driver to glance her way. His face was turned, so she couldn't get a good look at him. Yet there was something familiar about the set of his shoulders and the cut of his jaw.

*Shane?*

Lia gasped and started to move forward. But her feet felt as if they were filled with concrete. Before she could break free, the light changed and the truck sped off.

*The license plate. Get the number.*

With her heart pounding Lia strained forward for a better look, only to stumble. She might have fallen if an older woman walking the opposite way down the sidewalk hadn't grabbed her arm and steadied her.

"Are you okay?"

Lia's hand moved protectively to her belly as she gazed into the concerned eyes of the older brown-skinned woman. "I—I'm fine."

She shot a quick glance down the street but the truck had disappeared.

"I know it's none of my business—" The Good Samaritan spoke in heavily accented English. She hesitated for a moment before continuing. "—but a woman in your condition shouldn't be wearing such high heels."

Her condition? Lia pulled her hand from her abdomen with what she hoped was a casual gesture. She resisted the urge to glance down at her belly. "I thought I saw someone I knew. I simply moved too fast."

Lia wondered how long this would keep happening. Four months and she was still seeing Shane around every street corner.

Last month Lia had thought she'd seen him at the grocery store. But when she'd hurried up to the tall, dark-haired man, the guy hadn't looked anything like him. Last week it had been in a restaurant. The guy with the thick dark hair that curled just above his collar had been seated with his back to her. With her heart pounding in her throat, she'd strolled by his table. On closer observation, she'd discovered the man looked nothing like Shane. Not only did he have brown eyes—instead of blue—but crooked teeth and a wedding ring.

And then there was the man in the truck today...

"Are you okay, miss?"

"I'm fine." Remembering her manners, Lia turned to the woman with a warm smile. "Thank you for coming to my assistance."

"God bless you." The woman cast a pointed glance to Lia's nearly flat belly. "And your *bebé*."

Lia offered up a wan smile as the woman hurried off. She hoped Miguel wouldn't have the woman's keen psychic abilities.

Being careful to watch for any cracks in the sidewalk, Lia took carefully measured steps on her trek to the door. She sensed the construction workers watching her, but didn't hear a single wolf whistle. She didn't know whether to be offended or relieved.

She exhaled when she finally reached the building. A blast of cool air greeted her as she opened the nightclub door and stepped inside.

The interior seemed to be very much a work in progress. The sounds of hammering and the whine of electric saws and drills filled the air. Lia's heart sank.

From the unfinished state of the interior, the opening had to be *many* months away. She clenched her purse firmly and told herself not to panic. It might still work out. Besides, she'd driven all the way over here. It would be foolish to leave without speaking with Miguel.

"May I help you?" A dark-haired man with a thick accent stepped in front of her. She wasn't sure if he was a security person, a supervisor or simply being helpful.

"I hope so." Lia flashed the man a smile. "I'm here to see Miguel Mendoza. I'd appreciate it if you could point me in the direction of his office."

He looked at her curiously, but didn't ask any questions. "All the offices are that way." He gestured with his head toward a closed door to the right. "Miguel's will be the last one on the right. I don't think he's left for lunch yet."

"Thank you." Lia had to skirt a couple sawhorses and a few power cords before reaching the door. When she opened it and saw painted walls and carpeted floors, her spirits rose.

An accountant could comfortably work in these conditions. Even if the club wasn't open and bringing in revenue, there were dozens of things she could do to help out.

"Please let me get this job. Please let me get this job. Please let me get this job," she murmured under her breath as she strode down the long hallway.

She stopped outside the last office on the right. Her hand paused on the knob when she heard voices coming from inside. She hesitated. The laughter she heard told her she wouldn't be interrupting a meeting but perhaps she should wait...

After a few more minutes of listening to muted conversation with an occasional burst of laughter thrown in, Lia squared her shoulders and rapped on the door.

"Come in."

Miguel sat behind a large desk. Dressed fashionably in a cream-colored shirt and brown pants, he was a handsome man with jet-black hair and dark brown eyes.

Both he and the man he'd been speaking with rose as she entered the room.

"I hope I'm not interrupting," she said softly, "but I wondered if you had a few minutes to talk."

"Natalia, it's been too long." A broad smile of welcome split Miguel's face, showing a mouthful of perfect white teeth. "How's Eric?"

"Ah, he's well." Lia glanced at the other man, who was watching the two of them with a speculative gleam in his eyes. She took a step backward. "If you're busy, I can wait."

"We've finished our business. Your timing couldn't be

more perfect." Miguel turned to the guy in the hard hat. "Juan, I'd like you to meet Natalia Serrano. Her brother Eric and I go way back."

Miguel completed the introductions and after a minute of polite conversation, Juan left.

"I hope I'm not interrupting your lunch plans." Lia sank into a plush leather chair positioned in front of the desk.

"Eric's baby sister is never an interruption." Miguel sat down, an easy smile on his lips.

Lia couldn't figure out why she was so nervous. This was Miguel, for goodness' sake. Growing up, he'd spent as much time at her house as he had at his. Back then, her friends had told her she was crazy not to try to get something going with him. But how could she when he'd always seemed like another brother to her?

"What brings you out this way?" he asked.

"Eric mentioned that you might be in the market for an accountant." Lia clutched the straps of the purse in her lap but managed to keep her voice casual and offhand. "If you remember, I got my degree in business with a concentration in accounting and finance. I'd been working as an accountant but got laid off in February. I could start immediately and—"

"Whoa." Miguel held up a hand. "Let me stop you before you go any further."

Heat shot up Lia's neck. She'd been chattering; just what you weren't supposed to do in an interview. *Let the prospective employer take the lead.* That was what all the articles she'd read had told her. Yet what had she done? Barged in without an appointment, then tried to control the conversation.

"I'd hire you in a second, Lia." Miguel's dark eyes met hers. "But I'm not looking at opening the doors until later this summer."

Lia thought of mentioning all the ways she could help until then, but she kept her mouth shut. Miguel was a smart guy. If he thought he'd be able to use her skills before the nightclub opened, he'd have said so.

"I understand." She cursed the slight quiver to her voice that she couldn't quite control. "Thanks for your time. I'd appreciate it if you'd keep me in mind when the job does come open."

She rose to her feet and headed toward the door, seeing no need to waste any more of his time.

"When would you be able to start?"

Lia's heart stopped. She turned slowly. "Today. I could start today."

"While *I* don't have anything, I was talking to Sawyer Fortune this morning."

He paused as if waiting for her response to the name.

"I don't know him." Though the Fortune name was well-known in Red Rock, Lia had never personally met any of the family. Not surprising since they hardly ran in the same social circle.

"Sawyer is the former director of publicity and marketing for JMF Financial. He's now running New Fortunes Ranch. It's out on the edge of town. Apparently his bookkeeper is on medical leave and he needs someone to replace her for a couple months. Perhaps longer." Miguel's eyes turned warm. "I could call and get you an interview. Put in a good word."

Lia blinked back unexpected tears. "I'd appreciate that very much, Miguel."

"It probably won't be the salary you're used to getting as an accountant," he warned. "But it would be a regular paycheck and good—"

"I'm sure it will be fine," Lia said quickly. "I need a job."

"Let me call him now." Miguel picked up his cell phone.

As they waited for Sawyer to answer, Lia hoped her luck had finally changed.

With the roar of planes landing and taking off in the background, Shane stowed his suitcase in the back of the extended-cab pickup then climbed inside. It was strange that returning to Red Rock should feel so much like coming home.

"Natalia has made life so much easier for me at the ranch," Sawyer told his older brother as they left the Red Rock airport. "Marjorie is a good bookkeeper but Natalia has a background in accounting."

When Shane had asked his brother how things were going at New Fortunes Ranch, he hadn't expected him to start raving about his temporary bookkeeper.

Shane smiled at his brother. "Speaking of women, are you still dating—"

Shane searched for a name but came up empty.

"No." Sawyer's voice was flat. "That was over long ago."

Just like him and Lia, Shane thought. Except that whatever was between them had been over without really getting started. Yet strangely, ever since their New Year's Eve encounter, she hadn't been far from his thoughts.

"Do you ever think of her?" Shane asked.

"Not at all." Sawyer cast him a glance, apparently puzzled by his brother's sudden interest in his social life.

"What about Natalia?" Shane teased. "You mentioned she was young and single. You're obviously smitten…with her work."

Sawyer chuckled. "You're forgetting one important fact. She's an employee. Even if she wasn't working for me, she keeps it all business."

"Meaning, you don't appeal to her. Perhaps she doesn't like men who smell like horses. Or perhaps she's immune to your newly acquired Texas charm?"

"Go ahead, rub it in, big brother."

Shane laughed. It was good to be home.

"What did you find out about Jeanne Marie?"

The smile disappeared from Shane's lips.

It had been the first question Sawyer had asked when he'd picked him up at the airport. Shane had put him off then and he planned to put him off now.

"Like I said, we'll get into all that when the entire family is together." When Shane had uncovered the truth about Jeanne Marie and her relationship with their father, he'd called Sawyer and asked him to get all their siblings together. "What time will everyone be at the ranch?"

"Eight o'clock." The irritated look on Sawyer's face told Shane his brother didn't appreciate being kept in the dark.

The truck slowed to a stop in front of the ranch house where Sawyer lived, a place Shane would now call home, too. The white clapboard structure, sheltered from the midday sun by the leafy branches of a mammoth cypress tree, projected an air of welcome that eased the tension in Shane's shoulders. He'd just stepped from the vehicle when Sawyer's cell phone beeped. He glanced down at the text then up at Shane. "Natalia has a question regarding an account. Would you like to come with me and meet her?"

Shane really wasn't in the mood to socialize but he was curious about the woman who'd impressed his brother. "Sure."

"Just leave your luggage in the truck." Sawyer tossed the words over his shoulder as he hopped out. "We can pick it up on our way back to the house."

Shane followed his brother to a small nondescript building between the main house and the bunkhouse. Someone had planted wildflowers out front and had hung several hanging planters of bright red geraniums from the eave. He lifted a brow. "Flowers?"

"Natalia asked if she could plant them. Apparently she likes to garden and she lives in an apartment. I figured as long as I don't have to do anything with them, she can plant an orchard if she wants," Sawyer replied in a somewhat defensive tone.

"They look nice." Shane found himself even more intrigued by the woman who was his brother's new bookkeeper. The one who'd been unmoved by Sawyer's easy charm.

Sawyer pushed open the door and a tinkling of bells sounded.

"I got your text," Sawyer said.

"You didn't need to rush over." The muffled female voice that responded sounded oddly familiar.

Shane followed his brother into the room. The woman's back had been to them, but then she swiveled in her chair to face them. When he saw those big brown eyes, he felt as if he'd been kicked in the chest.

"Lia," he managed to croak out. His heart leaped the same way it had when their eyes had met across the crowded ballroom all those months ago.

She looked just as beautiful as he remembered with all that thick dark hair and red pouty lips. Instead of a form-fitting dress like she'd worn the last time he'd seen her, she wore lots of multicolored layers that gave no hint of the curves beneath. But Shane knew those curves well. Remembered how they'd felt beneath his fingers.

Lia shook her head as if trying to clear it. "Shane?" She blinked once. Then blinked again. "Is it really you?"

Clearly confused, Sawyer's gaze remained focused on her. "You know my brother?"

Lia's mouth opened then closed. Shane could almost see the wheels in her head turning, trying to decide how much to divulge.

"Lia and I have met." Shane kept his tone easily matter-of-fact. "In fact, you could say we're old friends."

His eyes dared her to disagree.

She stiffened. A smile that didn't quite reach her eyes formed on her lips.

It was apparent she hadn't forgiven him. Heck, he hadn't forgiven himself. There were so many other ways he could have handled the situation. Rather than just abruptly telling her he was leaving Red Rock and wasn't sure he'd be back, he could have told her he had family business to handle. Important business that would keep him away from Red Rock for an indeterminate amount of time. But he could have assured her he was interested in seeing her again when he did return.

He could have asked for her contact information so they could keep in touch. Could have explained he would eventually be moving to Red Rock and had only booked the hotel room for convenience. But he hadn't. He'd let her walk out of that room as if the night they'd shared meant nothing, as if *she* had meant nothing to him.

He wanted to make it right. He wanted to explain himself.

"I'm tied up with some stuff tonight," Shane said. "But I'd like to take you to dinner tomorrow. We could go to the Red Rock Country Club and catch up."

Shane could feel his brother's curious stare. Once they were alone Sawyer would be demanding answers. But Lia was his focus right now, not his brother.

He sensed her unease. He wished he could reassure her that there was no way he was sharing details about what had happened between them on New Year's Eve with his brother. When they had dinner, he'd make sure she understood she could trust him to keep his mouth shut.

"What do you say, Lia?" Shane prompted. "Will you go to dinner with me?"

For a second he thought she might decline his invitation. Then she smiled. "Sounds like fun."

But when her eyes met his, the silent message in those dark depths warned that, before there would be any "fun," he had a lot of explaining to do.

## Chapter Four

The family summit that night was held in Sawyer's living room. Shane's three other brothers and sister had arrived shortly before eight and now gathered in the large room with the whitewashed walls, open beams and oversize comfortable furniture.

The simmering tension slapped Shane in the face as he walked into the room. There was a lot at stake tonight for all of them. Not only in terms of the family business but personally, as well.

Their parents, James Marshall and Clara Fortune, had been married for over thirty years. While the marriage had not been without strife, Shane's mother had always seemed to understand and tolerate his father's moods.

Clara had recently gone back to school to finally earn her college degree and with her five children now out of the nest, she seemed relatively happy and content. She was also, as far as Shane knew, oblivious to the fact that her husband had sold off a majority share of JMF Financial stocks and given it to a woman named Jeanne Marie.

As the oldest, Shane had thought about telling his mother what he and his siblings had discovered. But when he had discussed doing that with his brothers and sister, they felt they should keep quiet until they had more answers.

While Shane still didn't know what was really going on, he knew a heckuva lot more now than he knew back in January. The news he brought with him tonight would rock his siblings' world.

His brother Wyatt had shown up tonight in jeans and boots, looking more like a cowboy than a vice president of JMF Financial. When Shane had razzed the easygoing Wyatt about his upcoming marriage to Sarah-Jane Early, his brother had responded quite seriously he hoped Shane would one day be so lucky.

Asher, the second oldest, sat quietly talking to Sawyer. He had chimed in that it was all about finding the right woman. For Asher, that woman was his fiancée, Marnie McCafferty. After his divorce last year, he'd gotten full custody of his four-year-old son, Jace, who was now being entertained by the housekeeper in the other room.

Though Sawyer was still ostensibly the director of publicity and marketing for the family firm, he, too, had embraced ranching and his new life in Red Rock.

Victoria was the youngest of his siblings. Now living permanently in Red Rock, Victoria had married Garrett Stone last year and together they ran Pete's Retreat animal sanctuary.

"What did you find out?" Victoria demanded, fixing her gaze on him. Even as a little girl, she'd never been known for her patience.

The other siblings stopped talking and focused on Shane.

His heart felt like a leaden weight in his chest. He'd always looked up to his father. While his dad was by no means perfect, Shane had admired and respected him.

He'd believed his father to be an honorable man. Now it appeared that his trust had been misplaced.

"You're not going to like this." Shane raked his hand through his hair. "I found Jeanne Marie." The name felt awkward on Shane's tongue.

Wyatt's brows slammed together. "Did you speak with her?"

"What does she look like?" Victoria asked.

Asher leaned forward in the large chair, resting his forearms on his thighs. "How old is she?"

Shane raised his hand and waited until they quieted and all eyes were on him. He reminded himself this wasn't about money. It was about family.

"She's living in Arkansas. She goes by the name Jeanne Marie Fortune." Shane took a deep breath. "It appears our father is a bigamist."

"Did you see a marriage certificate?" Wyatt asked.

Shane shook his head. "But what other explanation could there be? She's using his last name."

Victoria gasped. "There has to be some mistake."

"It's dangerous to make assumptions, Shane," Sawyer warned, though his brows were furrowed with worry. "We need to talk to Dad. Hear what he has to say."

"Mother needs to be told of this right away," Wyatt asserted.

"It's going to be hard to speak with either one." Shane stood, unable to sit any longer. "They've been out of the country for several weeks. I'm sure Dad taking Mom away isn't a coincidence. I think he figured out I was close to learning the truth and that's why they left on this vacation."

"Do we know when they'll be back?" Asher asked.

"The last time I checked with Dad's personal assistant she insisted she didn't know." Shane hadn't believed Beverly, but he could hardly call her a liar. "Their absence may actually work to our advantage."

"How do you figure?" Sawyer looked confused.

"I've invited Jeanne Marie to come to Red Rock for a visit."

"Are you crazy?" Wyatt's voice rose.

Victoria's eyes flashed. "If she's having an affair with Daddy, I don't want her here."

"We should talk with Dad before we speak with this woman," Sawyer insisted again, his jaw jutting out in a stubborn angle.

"Look—" Shane kept a hold on his temper with both hands, reminding himself he'd had time to sort all this through in his head. He needed to give his siblings time to process this, as well. "I think we can all agree that we've gotten nowhere trying to get information from our father."

He glanced around the room and waited until he saw each of them reluctantly nod. "That's why I felt it was imperative to go to the source. Once I located her, I called and told her I was James's son. I said the family wanted to get to know her."

"How did she react?" Wyatt asked quietly.

"Yes." Victoria leaned forward in her seat. "What did she say? Was she shocked to hear from you? Apologetic? I hope she was embarrassed."

"She seemed surprised and strangely happy to hear from me." Shane had been amazed when she'd greeted him like a long-lost relative.

"That's weird," Victoria said.

His sister was right. It made no sense. Shane began to pace, the unsettled feeling he got whenever he thought of Jeanne Marie welling up inside him. "She accepted my invitation immediately. Not one bit of hesitation."

"When will she be here?" Sawyer asked in a quiet voice Shane had to strain to hear.

A knot formed in the pit of Shane's stomach. "A few weeks."

"What if Mom and Dad are back by then?" Victoria asked, an uncharacteristic tremble in her voice.

"Then they're back," said Wyatt with a grim look on his face. "I don't like the fact that we've kept this from Mother as long as we have. She has a right to know."

"But know what?" Sawyer's blue eyes flashed. "We aren't certain who this Jeanne Marie is or what she wants."

"We know she's calling herself a Fortune," Shane said through gritted teeth. "We know that our father gave her half of the shares of JMF Financial at the beginning of the year."

"And we know he won't talk to us about her," Victoria added quietly, "even when we ask."

"The way I see it, we have no choice but to find out what we need to know from her," Shane continued.

"Shane is right," Asher said in a soft, Southern drawl. "We have to discover the truth. We can't go on not knowing."

"In just a few weeks, we'll have our answers," Shane said. And when he glanced around the room at the worried faces of his siblings, he realized that day couldn't come soon enough for any of them.

Lia dressed carefully for her dinner with Shane. Though she had a lot of fashionable clothes in her closet, several suitable for dinner at the country club, most of them didn't fit.

She'd barely gained any weight yet, but the tiny pooch had rendered most of her formfitting clothes unwearable. After trying on a dozen dresses and skirts, she finally settled on a chic tunic dress in navy. For tonight, she grabbed a pair of low-heeled sandals in silver, glancing wistfully at all the higher-heeled ones in her closet.

A knock at the door sounded just as Lia finished tossing a few essentials into a silver clutch. She'd told Shane she could meet him at the country club but he'd insisted on picking her up.

It wasn't that she was trying to save him a trip into town—she simply wasn't sure how he was going to react to the news that he was going to be a daddy. If things got ugly, she'd prefer to have her own transportation.

"Just a minute," she called out when a knock sounded again. After one last quick glance in the mirror she forced herself to walk slowly across the room. Her heart was beating fast enough.

Though she was almost positive it was Shane at the door, she took a second to glance through the peephole before unfastening the security chain and flipping the dead bolt.

"Hi," she said in welcome as she opened the door.

Shane stepped inside and glanced back at the door. "Quite the security setup you've got going."

"A girl living alone in this neighborhood can't be too careful." Lia kept her tone light. She didn't mean to badmouth her home. She was lucky she had a place to live. And she liked her neighbors, which was more than many people could say. "Let me make sure all the lights are off then I'm ready to leave."

Since the apartment was only three rooms, that didn't

take long. She could see Shane taking in the place where she lived. Though nothing showed on his face, from the way his gaze lingered on the threadbare carpet and the walls in desperate need of repainting, it was obvious he wasn't impressed.

"It may be small, but I have a roof over my head." Lia knew he'd never understand the significance of the words. Until she'd gotten the job working for Sawyer, she'd worried she might have to accept her mother's offer and move to Boston. Either that or live out of her car.

"A roof is always a good thing," he said smoothly, opening the door for her.

Even though he was dressed much more casually than the first time they'd met, he looked just as fabulous in khaki pants and a navy blazer. His hair was perfectly cut and styled. Lia wanted to ask him if he always looked so put together.

She caught a tantalizing whiff of cologne as she strolled past him. Thankfully smells no longer made her nauseated like they had those first couple months of her pregnancy.

They discussed the weather on the way to the car—how hot it had been lately even though it wasn't technically summer yet. Lia didn't mind chatting about the mundane. It was as if they were attempting to find their way back to the ease they'd experienced back in his hotel suite.

It was as though this was their first "date." Which in a way it was, she realized. When he opened the door to the sleek black Mercedes parked at the curb, she felt like a princess on her way to the ball.

"You changed jobs," he said as the car surged away from the curb with a low purr.

"The year started out a little rocky for me," Lia admitted.

He slanted a sideways glance in her direction. "What happened?"

*Other than finding out I was pregnant on Valentine's Day and then losing my job two weeks later?*

She shrugged. "The small manufacturing company I was working for began laying off employees right after the first of the year. I survived the initial round of cutbacks but lost my job the beginning of March."

"I'm sorry to hear that." Shane sounded genuinely sincere. "How do you like working for Sawyer?"

"I like it." Though the work wasn't nearly as challenging as what she'd done in her past position, she was thankful to have the regular paycheck. "It's a nice relaxed atmosphere and Sawyer is a great boss."

She couldn't have said what they talked about on the short drive out of town. But when he turned into the winding drive leading up to the country club, Lia felt her stomach clench.

Minute by minute it was getting close to the time when she would have to tell him her news. She wasn't sure what he would say, how he would react.

He'd be shocked of course. She'd been stunned when she'd done the pregnancy test. In fact, she'd gone out and bought two more and taken them, too, just to be sure.

Of course, she knew that taking antibiotics for her sinus infection had lessened the pill's effectiveness. But they'd used condoms. Each time. It had been hard for her to believe she'd gotten pregnant from that night, even after a doctor's exam had confirmed the test results.

An older gentleman that Lia recognized from her neighborhood stood at the door, looking dapper in a perfectly pressed uniform. She smiled at him as he opened the door for her and Shane.

Lia had been in the Red Rock Country Club a handful

of times, mostly for special events. She remembered the white plastered walls, all the beautiful dark wood and the extensive windows in the dining room that afforded an amazing view of the golf course.

And, of course, the flowers. They were everywhere. Large arrangements with a myriad of petals in vibrant colors that looked too perfect to be real but smelled too good to be dried.

Though Lia would have preferred a more secluded spot for her discussion with Shane, was there really a perfect time or place for what she had to say?

The question was, what kind of response would she receive to her announcement? It was sad that she didn't know him well enough to know how he would react. She knew what she hoped he'd say. That he wanted to be a part of their child's life. That while it wasn't good timing, a new life was something to be celebrated.

The maître d' led them to a table by the window. Lia was pleased that, because of the way the tables were situated, they had a surprising amount of privacy.

"The wine list, sir," the maître d' said as he presented it to Shane with a flourish.

"I don't care for any wine this evening," Lia said quickly.

Shane smiled. "Perhaps a glass of champagne?"

"You remembered." She couldn't help being pleased.

"Of course," he said smoothly. "I remember everything about our time together."

He asked again about the champagne when the waiter arrived but didn't press when she said she'd stick with tap water.

"How have you been?" Lia asked when the waiter slipped away to get Shane's glass of wine. "Did you get your family business taken care of?"

He stilled. "Family business?"

"You told me you had some family business to take care of when we were last together." She gave a little laugh and waved a hand in the air. "Of course that was months ago. I'm sure it's all squared away by now."

"Actually, it's not," Shane replied. "But we're making progress."

Lia took a sip of water. *Ticktock.* The clock in her head ticked down the minutes until she told him her news and this pleasant interlude would come to an end. "Are you in town for long?"

"I'm relocating to Red Rock." Shane's expression turned brooding. "My brothers and sister are all here. We're a close-knit group."

"What about your parents?"

"They still live in Atlanta."

"I bet you miss them." Lia sighed. "My mother now lives in Boston. I can't tell you how much I wish she was closer."

"My parents travel a lot." Shane's eyes took on a distant look.

"Are you close?"

He appeared surprised by the question. Normally she'd never have asked, but there'd been a hesitancy in his voice and an almost sad look in his eyes when he mentioned them.

"Are you close to your parents?" she repeated when he didn't answer.

"I used to be." He shifted his gaze to the waiter as he set Shane's wine before him and waited for his approval. Shane took a sip then nodded.

The waiter melted away and Shane returned his attention to Lia. "My mother is a wonderful woman. My father is hardheaded but I always thought he was a good man."

Lia picked up the change in tense immediately. "You no longer think so?"

Shane took another sip of wine then smiled. "Let's not talk about my family tonight. Let's talk about you. Are you still doing the beadwork?"

A ripple of pleasure traveled through her body. He remembered that, as well.

"I am," she said. "In fact, the money I made from it kept me going during the two months I was laid off."

"I can't believe you couldn't find work as an accountant."

"Not in Red Rock. If I'd gone much longer without a position, I'd have started looking in San Antonio. But this is home and I like it here. Commuting doesn't really appeal to me. And relocating, even when you don't have much stuff, can be expensive."

"Have you thought what you're going to do when Sawyer's bookkeeper comes back from medical leave?"

*Have a baby,* Lia thought.

It was something she tried not to think about. The last update she'd received was that the woman was supposed to be gone until late July.

"I'll find another job." Lia sounded much more positive than she felt. "Miguel Mendoza is opening a nightclub later this summer. He's a friend of my brother Eric. He promised to keep me in mind for an office position." Lia reached for her glass, almost knocking it over. "He's also a marketing executive for Home Run Records. You may have met him through that position."

"Are you and Miguel…close?"

"You mean, have we ever dated?" Lia shook her head. "He's always been like another brother to me. Besides, he recently married Nicole Castleton—you know, the heiress to the boot company? They were high school sweethearts and got back in touch."

"I'm so happy I ran into you again." Shane took her hand, playing with her fingers.

His touch did strange things to her insides and brought all those feelings from that long-ago night flooding back.

"Definitely fate at work," she said lightly, sounding breathless.

He sniffed the air appreciatively. "You're wearing Chanel tonight."

"I can't believe you remembered."

"You're not that easy to forget." Shane caressed her palm with his thumb. "I'm glad you accepted my invitation for dinner, because I wanted a chance to apologize for how it ended between us."

"You don't have—" she began, but he continued as if she hadn't even spoken.

"I should have made it clear how much I enjoyed our time together and that I really did want to see you again."

"You were leaving town," she said, her voice sounding faint even to her ears. "That's what you said. That you had business elsewhere."

"All true," he said, his eyes clear and very blue. "But I felt a real connection with you. I think of what I *could* have done, *should* have done, *wished* I'd done to make sure we kept in touch, and I'm consumed with regret."

His words buoyed her sagging spirits. Until now, she had thought she'd been the only one who had wished things had gone differently that morning.

Lia had planned to wait until after dinner to mention the baby, but he'd opened his heart to her and bared his soul. It was time she did the same. "I have something I've wanted to tell you, too."

He smiled. "Anyone ever tell you that you're cute when you're serious?"

A warmth crept up Lia's neck. She moistened her dry lips with the tip of her tongue.

Heat flared in his eyes.

"This is important."

The slight tremor in her voice brought a faint frown of concern to his forehead.

"No worries." The gentle kindness in his tone was nearly her undoing. "You can tell me anything."

Before Lia could get a single word past her suddenly stiff lips, his phone buzzed. Casting an apologetic look at her, he pulled the ultra-slim black phone from his pocket and glanced at the screen. He grimaced. "I'm sorry but I need to take this. It shouldn't take long."

He stood and exited the dining room, the phone pressed against his ear.

Lia exhaled the breath she didn't realize she'd been holding. Perhaps she should be grateful she'd been granted a slight reprieve.

The only problem was, it was temporary. Because the news that she had for Shane was something he needed to hear. And he needed to hear it tonight.

## Chapter Five

Shane shoved the phone into his pocket. If it hadn't been Jeanne Marie, he wouldn't have taken the call. But if the woman was backing out of her agreement to come to Red Rock, he needed to know about it so he could change her mind.

Thankfully she simply wanted to tell him she'd booked her flight and to give him the itinerary.

Shane rubbed the back of his neck. Jeanne Marie was a puzzle. She seemed so darned happy to be coming to Red Rock to meet the family. Didn't she realize his father had a wife? And that all the people she was coming to meet would view her as a home-wrecker?

He blew out a harsh breath, his good mood of a few minutes ago soured. Now that he knew the reason for her call, he wished he'd let voice mail pick up.

Shane paused at the doorway to the dining room, settling his gaze on Lia, who sat staring out the window with a pensive look on her face. She was as pretty as he remembered with her thick dark hair and those big brown eyes. Tonight she wasn't showing nearly as much skin as she had the night they'd met and, like yesterday, her dress was loose and almost shapeless.

She had a cute figure. He'd like to see her flaunt it a bit more. Still, she appealed to him as much as she did all those months ago.

Though he didn't know Lia well, he could tell when he picked her up that something was troubling her.

Something troubled him, too...the dump she lived in. Though he wasn't that familiar with Red Rock, he got the impression most of the town was fairly nice. But as he'd driven closer to where she lived, the upscale community flavor had taken a dramatic turn.

On Lia's block, small groups of men sat on porch steps or stood on street corners talking. Little kids played in the street with no adult supervision. And her apartment...

He winced. The walls in the stairwell had been soiled and an overpowering odor of garbage filled the air. He hated to see so many locks on her door, though he'd been happy to see her taking measures to protect her own personal safety.

As he crossed the dining area, he wondered if one of his siblings might know of a place for rent that would be within Lia's price range. He made a mental note to ask them the next chance he got.

"Sorry that took so long." He slid into his seat and dropped the linen napkin back on his lap.

While he'd been gone, the waiter had brought out their salads: mixed greens with cranberries, blue cheese crumbles and candied walnuts.

"You didn't need to wait for me," he said, glancing at her untouched plate.

"I'm too nervous to eat," she said, then blushed at the admission.

That was right—she'd said she had something to tell him.

He wondered suddenly if she was in a relationship. Was that what she was finding so difficult to tell him? It made sense considering she was a beautiful woman.

Possibly she'd gotten back with her ex-boyfriend. The minute the thought crossed his mind, he discarded it. Shane prided himself on being a good judge of character. His first impression of Lia was of a strong, independent woman. He couldn't see her going back to a man who had cheated and lied to her.

He searched her troubled gaze. "Do you think you'd feel better if you get whatever is bothering you off your chest?"

She nodded. "I'm not a big believer in secrets."

"I'm not, either." Shane clenched his jaw, thinking of his father and all the lies. All the pain his dad's secrets had caused the family. All the pressure it had put on Shane as COO of JMF Financial. Unlike his siblings, he was having difficulty walking away from the company he'd been groomed to run. A company he loved.

"Shane." She paused for a second then took a deep breath and began again. "Shane. I'm pregnant. You're the father."

His eyes widened. Then he began to laugh. "Good one, Lia," he said. "That got my attention. Now, tell me what's troubling you."

Her brows pulled together in confusion. "I *am* pregnant. You *are* the father."

The look in her eyes brought his laughter to a halt. He inhaled sharply. "You can't be serious."

She lifted her chin. "I wouldn't joke about something this important."

When Shane had been ten, his brother Wyatt had deliberately jumped in front of him and he'd fallen off his bike, knocking the air from his lungs. He remembered how he'd felt. Stunned. Angry. He felt the same way now.

He hadn't expected this from Lia. Obviously he wasn't a good judge of character after all. A coldness swept across his body.

"I don't know what kind of game you're playing." He gripped the edge of the table with both hands and leaned forward, pinning her with his gaze. "We both know that what you're alleging is impossible. Even if you weren't on the pill, we used condoms."

He'd made sure of it that night. He *always* made sure. Even if a woman said she was on the pill, he wanted all bases covered. He spoke slowly and distinctly, making sure she understood he was nobody's fool. "Explain to me how a pregnancy is possible under those circumstances."

"I was taking antibiotics for a sinus infection, which, according to my doctor, lowered the pill's effectiveness." Lia stumbled over the words. "I know this is a shock. It was for me, too. When I took the test—"

"Explain to me how a pregnancy is possible under those circumstances," he repeated.

"I can't." Lia ducked her head, looking miserable. "All I know is I'm pregnant and the baby is yours."

"Are you sure it's not Doug's?" Did she really think he would have forgotten about her *boyfriend?*

Lia cocked her head, the look of confusion in her eyes Oscar-worthy. "Who's Doug?"

"Your boyfriend." A simmering anger fueled the sharp bite to his words. "The one you said cheated on you."

"Oh." Light dawned in her eyes. "You mean David."

"Whatever." Shane waved a dismissive hand. "How can you be certain the baby isn't his?"

"He and I, well, we hadn't been…together in that way

since November." Two bright spots of red dotted her pale cheeks.

"Or so you say." His gaze bored into hers. "What does Doug do for a living?"

"His name is—" Lia stopped herself midsentence and appeared to refocus. "Why does his occupation matter?"

"Please answer the question."

"He works for his uncle who has a car dealership."

Another sharp stab of disappointment lanced Shane's heart even though the answer was what he'd expected. "Financially it would be a whole lot better for you to pass your baby off as a Fortune rather than the son or daughter of a car salesman."

Lia's brows pulled together. "You never told me your last name. I didn't even know you were a Fortune until you walked into the office yesterday and Sawyer introduced you as his brother."

Shane made a scoffing sound. "You've been working for my brother for over a month."

"It's not as if Sawyer keeps family photos around—"

"Our families are well-known in Red Rock. Our pictures are always in the local paper."

Her chin jutted out. "Not yours."

"You probably already knew who I was when we got together on New Year's."

"Yeah, right," she said with exaggerated sarcasm. "That's why I went back to the hotel hoping to find out your last name. Do you have any idea how humiliating it is to be pregnant and not know the last name of your baby's father? And then to be stonewalled by the hotel staff as if I was some sort of stalker?"

"You went there with the goal of pinning this on me."

"My goal was to let you know you were going to be a father."

"Let's cut to the chase. I assume this is about money." His heart felt hollow, empty. He'd liked her. Had looked forward to getting reacquainted with her. Never had he expected her to try to shake him down. "If you were in a jam and needed help financially, all you had to do was ask. Instead you lied."

"I'm not lying." Tears flooded her eyes. "And I have a job now and one lined up later to take care of me and the baby."

The waiter hurried over, his gaze discreetly focused on the plates of food in front of them. "How are the salads, sir?"

"They're fine," Shane assured him, his tone all business. "Something has come up and we need to leave. You can put the meals on my brother's tab."

Lia rose to her feet, dabbing at her eyes with a tissue. They strode through the dining room without touching or speaking.

While waiting for the valet to retrieve the car, she turned to him. Her brown eyes, normally open and filled with good humor, were shuttered.

"I'm going to have the doorman call me a cab."

"You're not calling a cab." Shane forced a conversational tone. "Our discussion is just getting started."

She didn't respond but when the car pulled up, she stepped inside. Shane wasn't surprised. At this point nothing she could do or say would surprise him.

They were almost to her apartment before she spoke again. "I'm not lying. Whether you want to believe it or not, this baby is yours."

Shane tightened his hands on the steering wheel. He was ready to threaten her with a lawsuit if she kept spouting such nonsense, but a tiny niggle of doubt kept his mouth shut. What if the baby *was* his?

"I didn't grow up with a father around." Her voice shook slightly as she filled the silence. "That's why I was determined to find you. This baby will need you, Shane. Don't throw the opportunity away to get to know your son or daughter just because you're angry about the circumstances."

He thought of his brother Asher and his nephew Jace. Even when Asher was getting a divorce last year, he'd fought for full custody of Jace. Of course, Lynn had been a nightmare and a totally unsuitable parent.

His gut said Lia would be a good mother. Then again his gut had also told him she could be trusted.

Still, what if she was telling the truth? What if this child she was carrying was his?

"You've given me a lot to think about, Lia." This time Shane kept his conflicting emotions from his voice. "Tomorrow, my day is filled with meetings. Let's talk more on Thursday. I'll pick you up at nine and take you to breakfast."

"I'm afraid that time won't work." Lia shook her head, her voice filled with regret. "Thursday is a workday."

"I'll clear it with Sawyer," Shane said. "It won't be a problem."

"Are you sure?"

"Positive."

Relief crossed her face. "Then nine o'clock will be fine."

He wanted to tell her not to count her chickens yet. Tonight he'd figure out his strategy.

Tomorrow, he'd put that strategy into action.

Shane's brothers exchanged glances as he finished his story.

Wyatt shook his head. "Odds are the kid isn't yours."

"I never would have believed Natalia was capable of

something like this," Sawyer said, a distressed look on his face.

"Sounds to me like running into her on New Year's Eve may have been a setup," Asher said quietly.

Shane flexed his fingers and paced the area in front of the living room's large stone fireplace. "I considered the setup angle. But how was she to know that I'd wander out into the courtyard when I didn't even know it myself?"

"You said she caught your eye when you glanced into the ballroom," Wyatt reminded him. "Maybe she hoped if she went somewhere quieter and more private, you'd follow."

"It's possible." Shane raked a hand through his hair. "I can't believe this is happening."

Shane rarely swore but right now it fit his mood. Anger. Hurt. Betrayal. The emotions were woven so tightly together it was impossible to say where one ended and the other began.

"What are you going to do if the baby *is* yours?" Asher asked.

"I'll hire me the best damn lawyer and get full custody, just like you did with Jace." Shane spat out the words. He couldn't believe Lia had fooled him so completely.

"It's not easy being a single parent," Asher warned. "You may want to think twice about suing for complete custody."

"You guys are putting the cart before the horse." Wyatt blew out a breath and stood. "The kid probably isn't even his. Even if she wasn't on the pill, Shane said he used condoms every time. Right?"

His brother looked to him for confirmation and Shane nodded.

"So, we're wasting time talking about something that

isn't a concern." Wyatt cast him a glance. "I assume you have a plan?"

"I've got a plan." Shane's chuckle held no humor. "Tomorrow, Natalia Serrano will find out just what happens when you tangle with a Fortune."

## Chapter Six

Even though she didn't have to be at work at eight this morning, Lia still woke at her regular time. She quickly readied herself for the day ahead then stepped to her closet to decide what to wear.

It was a relief that she no longer had to keep her pregnancy a secret, especially when she had so many cute maternity dresses on loan from a girlfriend.

She pulled out a bold orange cotton twill dress that tied under her bust. Though it had little pizzazz on its own, when paired with black leggings and a pair of platform pumps, it popped.

*Just like my belly,* Lia thought with a smile, curving her fingers under the small mound, which now reached her belly button.

"You're growing bigger and stronger every day, *mi amorcito,*" she cooed in a soft, melodic tone. "I feel you move all the time now."

At her last visit the doctor at the medical clinic had told her that she should start to feel movements from the baby and that it would probably feel like gas bubbles.

*Gas bubbles.* Lia wrinkled her nose. "Butterfly wings, not gas bubbles."

When she'd felt the first wisp of a butterfly wing, she'd sat down and cried. Because the baby had seemed real to her. And because she'd been alone.

A knock sounded and she jumped.

*Shane.*

This time the quivering in her stomach didn't have a thing to do with the baby. It had to do with her child's tall, dark and very handsome father standing on the other side of that door.

Tuesday Shane had been shocked and clearly disbelieving, but she'd expected that initial reaction. Now that he'd had more time to think about it, hopefully he was ready to accept that he would soon be a father.

"I'll be right there," she called out, snatching her favorite spice-colored lipstick from the dresser and quickly applying it. Looking her best gave Lia confidence and today she would need it.

A sharp rap at the door sounded, followed quickly by another louder, more forceful knock. Her lips lifted in a rueful smile. She was beginning to realize Shane Fortune was not a patient man.

After peering into the peephole and confirming it was indeed him, she unlatched the chain, flipped the dead bolt and opened the door.

He had on a pair of gray pants and a blue-and-gray button-down shirt. The shirt made his eyes look like the lapis lazuli beads she'd purchased yesterday.

She forced a bright smile, hoping to get the morning off on a good note.

"You look…nice." His eyes widened then lingered on the belly bump that had been well hidden beneath yesterday's tunic dress.

"Thank you." She glanced down at her platform pumps. "I guess I should ask if we're walking to a café or driving. If we're walking I probably should change shoes."

His gaze followed hers. When it slowly lifted, it left a trail of fire in its wake. "We're driving."

"Good," she said. "Because I love these shoes."

"You like nice things."

It was an odd comment. Lia lifted one shoulder in a slight shrug. "I'm a woman. Of course I like nice things."

"Liking nice things the way you do, it's probably hard for you to live here." He glanced around the small space.

Lia didn't like her studio apartment well enough to defend it. She shrugged. "It's okay…for now."

"You have aspirations of a much grander scale."

"I'm ambitious," she said slowly. Was he worried she wouldn't take good care of their child? "Like I told you on New Year's Eve, someday I hope to support myself on my beading income alone."

He gave a grunt that told her nothing.

"Where did you have in mind to eat?" she asked as he held open her front door.

"I thought we'd take a drive to San Antonio this morning."

"Why?" Lia pulled her brows together. "There are several nice cafés not far from here. Why would we drive an hour simply to eat?"

He took her arm, holding her gently but firmly on the trip down the stairs. "There's a place I know on the River Walk that I thought you'd like."

Lia loved the network of walkways along the San Antonio River one story beneath downtown San Antonio. Lined with restaurants and shops, the two parallel sidewalks connected the major tourist sites in the city. "It sounds like fun. But I assume Sawyer only gave me the morning off, not the whole day. And we'd spend at least an hour driving there and back."

"Don't worry about Sawyer—"

"I have to worry about him," Lia said as she slipped inside the Mercedes sedan. "He's my boss," she reminded Shane while he settled himself behind the wheel.

"He gave you the day off." Shane hit the accelerator and the car leaped away from the curb. "With pay."

"I couldn't accept—"

"He knows we have a lot to figure out." Shane's gaze remained fixed straight ahead as he pulled onto a roadway that would take them to San Antonio.

"You told him about the baby." Lia had known this would happen, eventually. She'd just assumed he'd wait to tell his family until after their talk today.

"He'd find out soon enough anyway."

She thought how nice Sawyer had been to her all these weeks. "How did he react? What did he say?"

Shane's hands tightened on the steering wheel but his expression gave nothing away. "He was surprised."

"Was he angry I didn't tell him I was pregnant when he hired me?" She hated to press, but she needed to know what she'd be facing when she reported for work tomorrow.

"I don't believe he's concerned with that at all."

Still, the worry bubbling up inside Lia wasn't so easily assuaged.

"It shouldn't matter. Marjorie is supposed to be back the end of July and I'm not due until late September." Lia hoped Shane understood that her being pregnant wasn't going to affect the job she did for his brother.

He made a sound she took for agreement.

Lia folded her hands in her lap to still their trembling. "So do you want to talk about…things…now or wait until after that first cup of coffee?"

He slanted a sideways glance. "I think any baby discussion should wait until after you've seen the doctor."

"I have seen a doctor," Lia hastened to reassure him. She certainly didn't want him to think she hadn't been taking proper care of herself. "I've been going to the Red Rock Clinic monthly since the pregnancy was confirmed."

As The Fortune Foundation funded the clinic, Shane was well aware of the services it offered. But because of his family's prominence in the community, he preferred to have today's business conducted outside of Red Rock.

"I booked an appointment for you later this morning with Dr. Gray, a prominent ob-gyn in San Antonio."

"That's nice of you, Shane, really it is. But I don't have the money to—"

"I'll pay for it."

"Not to mention San Antonio is too far for me to go for monthly checkups," she continued as if he hadn't spoken.

"Let's start with this one visit," Shane said easily. "See what you think of her."

Lia thought for a moment. Shane getting this appointment for her was really a sweet thing to do. And she was due for another checkup. If she went in for the appointment today, she could have Dr. Gray send the record of this visit to the Red Rock Clinic and then skip her monthly check there.

"If it would make you feel better to have her take a look at me and the baby, I'll do it."

"Thank you."

She leaned over and rested her hand lightly on the sleeve of his oxford shirt. "Thank you for caring."

The morning sped quickly by. During the drive and

over breakfast, Shane seemed to make an effort to keep the conversation light and off the baby. She followed his lead.

Despite the casual chatter, an underlying tension hovered in the air like a dark cloud. Lia told herself Shane was simply concerned about the baby's health. That once the doctor confirmed all was well he would relax. That the fact he cared enough to make this appointment was an encouraging first step.

Still, remembering the intensity of his reaction to the news of her pregnancy, she couldn't help but worry he still had doubts.

The office in Westover Hills had plush carpet and a hushed calmness that was in sharp contrast to the Red Rock Clinic. There were always little ones running around the clinic, shrieking and jabbering in both English and Spanish.

Shane opened the door to the suite and gestured for her to step inside. Several obviously pregnant women sitting in the waiting area lifted their eyes from the magazines in their laps. An appreciative gleam filled their gazes when they saw the man beside her.

When Lia hesitated, Shane placed his hand gently on her back and kept it there while urging her forward across the waiting room.

"Shane Fortune." He handed a card to the receptionist. "We're here to see Dr. Gray."

The receptionist's gaze flickered over the card. She immediately rose from behind the counter. "Of course."

Seconds later, the door leading to the exam rooms opened and they were ushered back. "But the other women—"

"Dr. Gray is expecting us," Shane said in a pleasant conversational tone. "We have an appointment. Remember?"

Lia decided the other women must be here to see the

other doctors. There had been a whole list of names by the
door, with Dr. Gray's at the very top.

Instead of being taken to an exam room as Lia expected,
they were ushered into an office with a large oak desk, a
burgundy leather chair for the doctor and two large chintz
wingbacks.

Shane waited until she was seated then sat in the other
chair.

He'd barely sat down when the door opened. They both
sprang to their feet.

"Mr. Fortune." The petite brown-haired woman with the
bobbed hair and warm smile extended her hand to Shane.
"How nice to meet you."

When the doctor turned to her, Lia found herself struck
by the kindness in her eyes. The fortysomething doctor
wasn't old or stodgy as she'd feared. Lia liked her instantly.

"I'm Lia Serrano," she said as the doctor's hand closed
over hers. "It's a pleasure to meet you."

"The pleasure is mine. You look lovely in orange," Dr.
Gray commented. "It's the perfect color for your warm
skin tone."

Lia began to relax. Perhaps this visit wouldn't be so bad
after all. "Thank you."

"Please sit down." She waited for them to sit down before she stepped behind the desk. "We have a lot to discuss."

Lia cocked her head. "We do?"

The doctor looked at Shane. "Mr. Fortune, when you
made this appointment, I assumed she had been informed—"

"Please. Call me Shane."

The doctor shifted her gaze to Lia. "Did Mr. Fortune,
er, Shane, discuss the reason for your visit today?"

Lia nodded.

The doctor appeared relieved. Which made no sense to

Lia. Wouldn't any pregnant woman coming to an ob-gyn clinic expect an exam?

"Good. Even though amniocentesis is a relatively common procedure, it's not without risk." The doctor opened her mouth to continue but Lia spoke up.

"Amniocentesis?" She looked at Shane. "You didn't say anything to me about having an amnio."

"Remember we talked about you getting a thorough checkup," Shane said in a patronizing tone that set Lia's teeth on edge.

She met his unyielding gaze with an equally firm one of her own. "An amnio is not part of a routine checkup."

"You are correct, Lia." Dr. Gray's gaze shifted between her and Shane, as if trying to grasp the dynamics. "But Shane indicated there was some question about paternity. The test is ninety-nine percent accurate in telling us if he's the father."

"We'll also be able to find out if the baby is a boy or a girl," Shane added in a persuasive tone.

Lia ignored him and focused on the doctor. "You said the procedure isn't without risk. What are the risks?"

"We don't need to get into all that—" Shane began.

"Yes, we do." Lia shot him a narrow, glinting glance before refocusing on Dr. Gray.

"Lia is right. A patient must be fully informed before consenting to any procedure." The doctor leaned forward, resting her forearms on the desktop, her entire attention on Lia.

"Don't leave anything out," Lia told her, unconsciously resting her hand on her belly.

"I won't." Dr. Gray's blue eyes turned serious. "While amniocentesis is considered to be safe and is done almost two hundred thousand times a year, it *is* an invasive diagnostic test with potential risks."

Out the corner of her eye, Lia saw Shane stiffen.

"Miscarriage is the primary risk. Because we do a lot of them in our facility, the rate of miscarriage after amniocentesis is about one in four hundred. Also, although extremely rare, it is possible for the needle to come into contact with the baby."

Before the doctor had even finished Lia began shaking her head. "I won't agree to it."

Beneath his tan, Shane's face turned pale. "I didn't realize performing this test could cause a miscarriage."

"It's rare," the doctor said, "but it can happen."

"One in four hundred isn't rare. But even if it was one in a million, I still wouldn't agree." Lia's voice rose and broke. She crossed her arms across her chest and fixed her gaze on Shane. "There is absolutely no question in my mind that this baby is yours. If you have doubts, we can do a DNA test after the baby is born. But I won't put his or her life at risk just because you choose not to believe me."

Shane nodded agreement. "I should have asked more questions about the risks before bringing up this option."

"And you should have told me what you had planned," Lia sputtered.

"You're right again," he said, looking surprisingly contrite.

"Let's take a break." Dr. Gray rose. "Shane, you can wait here in my office. Lia and I will go into an exam room. I'll do a quick check so I can reassure you both that this pregnancy is on course."

Although Shane now stood, Lia remained sitting, her heart beating a salsa rhythm against her ribs. She didn't care how much money or power Mr. Shane Fortune had; she was not risking the life of her baby over an unnecessary test.

"Lia?" Dr. Gray gestured toward the door. "Will you come with me?"

She lifted her chin. "I'm not having an amniocentesis."

"Only an exam," the doctor assured her. "And perhaps an ultrasound, if that's okay with you. The ultrasound can confirm the pregnancy is progressing normally and see if you're on target with your delivery date. If the baby cooperates, we may also be able to get an idea of the gender."

Because of cost constraints the Red Rock Clinic only did one ultrasound early in the pregnancy. Lia had thought she'd have to wait until the baby was born to know whether she was having a boy or a girl. "That'd be great."

"Do you want Mr. Fortune to come back with you for the ultrasound?"

"I'll wait here." Shane spoke before Lia could respond.

Lia rose to her feet, ignoring Shane's outstretched hand. She lowered her voice as she walked past him. "You and I will talk more about this later."

"That was the plan," he said, rocking back on his heels.

She didn't bother to respond. In her mind the *plan* had been to figure out ways for him to be involved with this pregnancy. The *plan* had been for them to figure out how to co-parent this baby once he or she was born. The *plan* had not been to put their baby at risk.

Shane Fortune might be used to having people bend to his will, but he would not run roughshod over her. Not when her child's life was at stake.

## Chapter Seven

"I still don't know the truth." Shane slammed his fist against the table in the deserted Red restaurant and the silverware jumped. "And I won't know until the baby is born."

"Calm down," Asher said.

"Do you want me to fire her?" Sawyer asked.

"Fire her?" Shane shook his head. "God, no. That would only make everything worse."

The truth was, though Shane knew there was a good chance that Lia was scamming him, he'd felt sorry for her this afternoon…and responsible for her distress.

They'd had a pleasant morning. Even when he'd sprung the appointment on her, she'd been totally willing to go along with his request to have another doctor take a look at her. When Dr. Gray had detailed the risks of doing an amnio, Shane had been stunned. He didn't recall the doctor mentioning those risks when he'd first approached her about doing the test. As much as he wanted to know the truth, even if Lia had agreed to the procedure, he wouldn't have let her go through with it.

"Mr. Bingham," he heard one of his brothers say. "I'm happy you could meet us on such short notice."

Shane pulled his thoughts back to the present just in time to see the attorney, who'd been working with the family on some legal matters, take a seat at their table.

Tom Bingham reminded Shane of an overstuffed teddy bear with gray hair and a down-home friendliness. He couldn't help liking the guy. Where opponents made their mistake was in not realizing that beneath that "aw shucks" exterior was a skilled litigator with a razor-sharp legal mind.

"I didn't realize he was coming." Shane's gaze shifted from Sawyer to Asher.

"I ran into Tom this morning and thought it'd be good if you got some legal advice," Sawyer said smoothly. "I didn't mention him joining us because I wasn't sure he could make it."

Tom lifted his briefcase and laid it on the table. "I'm surprised you're having a meeting of such a sensitive nature in a public place."

"We're the only ones here," Sawyer responded, clearly irritated by the hint of reproach in the attorney's tone. "It's safe."

"Understood," Tom said, then shifted his gaze to Shane. "Mr. Fortune, I understand from your brother that you're being threatened with a paternity suit."

"That isn't exactly accurate." Shane took a sip of iced tea. "A woman I know is claiming that I'm the father of her unborn baby. She hasn't threatened anything...yet."

The attorney peered at him over the top of his silver-rimmed glasses. "Is it possible the allegation is true?"

"A slight chance," Shane acknowledged. "But not likely."

"Will she consent to having an amniocentesis done to determine definitively if you are her child's father?"

"No."

Tom lifted a brow. "No?"

Shane shook his head. "I had it all arranged. But when she heard there was a chance of miscarriage, she refused. She said that after the baby is born, she'll do a DNA test."

"Hmm." Tom took off his glasses and cleaned them with a handkerchief. "Has she asked you for money?"

Shane shook his head.

"Odd." The attorney settled the glasses back on his nose.

"What's odd?" Asher asked.

"If she's so certain your brother is the father that she'll agree to a DNA test after birth, you think she'd do one now so she could start cashing in."

"She didn't want to take the chance of losing the baby," Shane explained.

"Of course she didn't. If this baby she's carrying *is* your child, she's hit the mother lode."

The worry and fear in Lia's eyes when Dr. Gray was discussing the risks were too real to be faked. She hadn't been thinking of his money—she'd been concerned about her child.

His child?

*Maybe.*

"What would you suggest Shane do now?" Sawyer asked.

Shane shot his younger brother a quelling glance. He could speak for himself.

"Until you're certain the child is yours, you have no legal obligation to do anything. Once paternity is established, that's a different story."

"If the child is mine, I'll want full custody."

Asher opened his mouth then shut it.

"That may be, uh, difficult." Tom seemed to choose his words more carefully now, apparently sensing Shane's animosity. "But definitely not impossible," he hurriedly added when he saw Shane's scowl. "We'll simply have to prove she's an unfit mother."

Shane rubbed his chin. "That may be a problem."

"What makes you say that?" Tom asked.

"I think Lia will be a good mother."

The attorney shrugged as if it was of no consequence. "In this business perception often matters as much as reality. She doesn't have to be unfit. We just have to make a judge think she is. So the more information we can dig up on her, the easier my job will be."

"You're suggesting we hire a private detective to look into her background." Wyatt spoke for the first time.

"That would be a good start," the attorney said, then hurriedly added, "if your brother agrees. I have several I can recommend if he's interested."

"Anything else you'd suggest?" Shane wondered why it felt as if he was betraying Lia when all he was doing was protecting his own interests.

"Get close to her. Do whatever it takes to get her to trust you." A sardonic smile lifted the attorney's lips. "If the child is yours and she does fight for custody, we'll know all her weaknesses."

It had been forty-eight hours since Lia had seen Shane. She glanced unseeing at the numbers on the computer screen. The workday had ended but she couldn't summon up the energy to get out of the chair.

She wondered if there had been a better way to inform

him that, while she appreciated his desire to know for sure the baby was his, she could not take the risk.

The chilly atmosphere between them on the drive back from San Antonio told her he was upset with her. Well, she was upset with him, too. He shouldn't have sprung something like that on her. And she had to admit a part of her was hurt he'd thought she was lying about the baby's paternity. But if she were in his shoes, she'd have been skeptical, too. Even she had found it difficult to believe she'd conceived with all the precautions they'd taken that night.

She pushed her chair back from the desk and glanced down at her belly. "I guess you were simply meant to be, *mi amorcito.*"

"Hiding someone beneath your desk?"

Lia jerked her head up to find Shane leaning against the doorjamb, arms crossed, an amused look on his face.

Her heart did a triple flip. The tension that had turned his face to stone when he'd dropped her off after their jaunt to San Antonio had disappeared. Today, he reminded her of the charming guy she'd met in the courtyard all those months ago.

"What brings you to the ranch today?" she asked cautiously.

"I live here." Shane's easy smile held a hint of amusement. "It's not just Sawyer's home—it's mine, too."

"Oh" was all Lia could manage.

"I heard there's a jazz concert in one of the parks tonight. I thought we could go together."

Was he extending an olive branch? Or would the night be spent fending off attempts to convince her to have an amniocentesis? If the latter was the case, she'd rather stay at home, put her feet up and watch a television rerun.

"I'm not changing my mind about the amnio." She spoke

bluntly, rising to her feet with as much grace as she could muster. "If that's what this is about you can—"

"That's not what this is about at all." He crossed the room in several long strides. Tonight he looked more cowboy than business executive in his jeans, boots and cotton twill shirt open at the neck. But no less dangerous.

Through the grapevine she'd heard that after he and Sawyer had returned from a lunch meeting in Red Rock, the two brothers had spent the afternoon inspecting their property on horseback.

"You were right to refuse the amniocentesis," he said in a husky voice filled with emotion. "And I was wrong to ask. The risk isn't worth it."

She shot him a skeptical glance. "Are you saying you believe me?"

He hesitated only a second. "I honestly don't know what to believe. Until the baby is born and we do the paternity test, I'm willing to concede that it's *possible* I'm the father."

While it wasn't the total acceptance she'd hoped for, it was a start.

"I appreciate the fact that you're keeping an open mind," Lia said softly. Her lips quirked in a rueful smile. "I'd have doubts, too, if I were in your shoes."

His eyes widened in surprise.

"Don't look so startled." She chuckled. "You're not the only one blindsided by this pregnancy. I couldn't believe it, either. I didn't want to believe it."

He looked at her, *really* looked at her, as if he were seeing her for the first time. "The pregnancy changed your life."

The statement hung in the air between them.

"It will change both of our lives." Lia put her hand to her back, which had begun to ache from so much sitting.

"But I'm a firm believer that all things happen for a reason. Somehow, my having this baby is all part of God's plan."

"A lot of women in your situation wouldn't see it that way," he said in a conversational tone. "They might have chosen not to continue the pregnancy."

Her gaze shot to his. "Is that what you wished I'd done?"

Shane shook his head and the look in his eyes reassured her.

"Do you like jazz?" he asked abruptly and she remembered his earlier invitation.

"I like Louis Armstrong."

"Well, you won't hear him but there will be some up-and-coming jazz artists at the park tonight." Shane's tone turned persuasive. "I thought it'd be good for us to get better acquainted, to become more comfortable with each other. If this baby is mine—"

"It is."

"—then the better we know each other, the easier it will be to co-parent when the time comes." He rocked back on his heels. "Will you go with me?"

Lia sent a quick prayer of thanks heavenward. At least he was keeping an open mind. "What time do the festivities start?"

"Seven. Supposedly there will be food vendors, so we can eat there, too."

Lia glanced down at her navy dress and heels. "I'll need to go home and change."

"I'll stop by your place around seven."

"Sounds good. And, Shane—"

"Yes?"

"Thanks for reaching out." The smile wobbled on her lips. "It means a lot."

* * *

When Lia opened the door that evening, Shane noticed the dress and heels were gone, replaced with a pair of white shorts and a sleeveless shirt in a wild-animal print. She looked cute, young and, without her heels, impossibly petite.

He'd forgotten how small she was, and a sudden protective instinct reared. Whether the baby was his or not, Lia would be facing a different future. Or, at the very least, different from the one she'd planned for herself.

Since the park was within walking distance of Lia's apartment, they decided to leave his car in the secured lot behind her building.

"How tall are you?" He took her arm as they started down the stairs.

"Five foot three."

He gave her a disbelieving look.

"I am." She drew herself up to her full height. "In fact, I'm actually five-three and a half."

His lips twitched. "Is that like being twelve and a half?"

She laughed, a silver tinkling sound, and pleasure lit up her entire face. "Yeah, kinda like that."

The streets around the park in downtown Red Rock had been barricaded off, allowing vendors to set up individual booths. Residents sat on lawn chairs and blankets on the grounds surrounding the bandstand. Many had brought picnic baskets filled with food and bottles of wine.

While looking for a good spot, they ran into several people Lia knew. Some spoke to her in Spanish while others conversed in English.

"You're bilingual," he said, sounding surprised.

"What was your first clue?"

"Are you going to raise your baby to be bilingual?"

*My baby?* she wanted to say. *It's your child, too.*

Small steps, she reminded herself. The fact that he was with her now and they were talking about the baby was encouraging.

"Actually, I've done some research on the topic." Lia waved to a woman she used to work with before returning her attention to Shane. "Studies suggest that children raised to be bilingual show positive cognitive benefits, including early reading and improved problem-solving skills."

He simply nodded as if she'd said the price of gasoline was set to take another hike upward.

She tugged him to a stop. "What do you think?"

Puzzlement filled his eyes. "What do you mean, what do I think?"

"This will be your child, too," Lia reminded him. "Do you have any concerns about my plan?"

For a second, Shane was struck speechless. His initial impulse was to say that they should wait to see if the baby was even his before getting into any heavy-duty parenting discussions.

From the beginning, Shane had been concerned about the liability of giving Lia the impression that he believed this was his child. Tom had told him not to worry.

The bottom line was, either the DNA would show he was the father or it wouldn't. According to the attorney, the only item on his agenda right now was getting to know Lia better.

"Exposing the baby to both languages sounds like a good plan." Shane took her arm and steered them around a group of rowdy cowboys, shielding her with his body.

Lia's gaze grew thoughtful. "Six months ago, developing a baby's language skills was the furthest thing from my mind."

"Before we reconnected—" Shane deliberately kept his

tone casual and offhand "—did you ever think about giving the baby up for adoption?"

It was an important piece of information. If she'd seriously considered that option, she might be more open to giving him full custody if the baby turned out to be his.

Lia responded to a greeting from a family gathered around a platter of tamales, but the smile on her face appeared strained. "When I found out I was pregnant, a lot of thoughts went through my head."

Shane noticed she hadn't answered his question directly. But he didn't press. He didn't want to do or say anything that might make her shut down completely. "Did you suspect you were pregnant before you took the test?"

"I'd missed my period, which was unusual, but I was under a lot of stress at work." She slanted him a sideways glance. "I suspected I was going to get laid off. I convinced myself that was the cause of my irregularity."

"You were trying to keep up the pretense that everything was okay." Shane thought of his father. Until his dad had given Jeanne Marie the shares of stock, he and his siblings hadn't been aware the woman existed.

"Then I started having morning sickness. I was tired all the time." Lia grimaced. "When I missed my second period I went out and bought a test. When the first test showed positive, I bought two more just to be sure."

"Did you say anything to Doug?"

Lia narrowed her gaze. An icy chill suddenly filled the air. "Why would I say anything to him?"

*Uh-oh.*

"I assumed that, by the time you discovered you were pregnant, he'd have realized what he lost and had come crawling to you, wanting you to take him back." Shane kept his eyes focused on the musicians, getting ready to start a new set.

The tension in the air dissipated like a balloon losing air.

"You're right. He did call. Said he wanted to try again. I made it clear I had no interest in a man who lied and cheated. I didn't mention the baby because I didn't see it was any of his business. I'm not particularly proud of being unmarried and pregnant. I know it happens all the time in today's society. But it doesn't happen in my family." Her lips twisted. "I didn't even tell my mother until a couple weeks ago."

Shane wanted to at least find out Doug's last name. But she'd effectively changed the direction of the conversation, making it impossible to go back without raising suspicions.

"How'd your mother take the news?"

"She was disappointed." Lia expelled a shuddering breath. "She thought she'd taught me better."

Anger surged in Shane. "We used every precaution."

"I mentioned that to her. I think what was hardest for her to accept was that I'd had a one-night stand and I didn't even know the man's last name."

"You told her that?"

"It was the truth. I'd tried to find you but the hotel stonewalled me. The fact you stayed in the Lone Star Suite that night had been my only lead."

"You must have been desperate." Sympathy rose up inside him but he shoved it down. "Were you worried how you were going to manage to support a baby all on your own?"

Lia glanced at the ground. "I told myself God would provide, but it got harder to keep the faith when I lost my job and then as my savings began to dwindle."

"There are families out there looking for a child to love." Shane gently steered the conversation back to adoption.

"I had a couple friends encourage me to go that route."

Lia expelled a heavy sigh. "But no one could possibly love this baby as much as I do."

There it was, laid out in front of Shane like a hog on a roasting spit. Not the answer he'd hoped for, but now he knew for certain what he'd suspected was true.

If this baby *was* his, a custody battle could easily end up being a brawl. Because Lia wouldn't be one to walk away from her child…no matter how much money he threw at her.

## *Chapter Eight*

Lia caught sight of Shane's brothers before they saw her. She and Shane had snagged a prime spot beneath the leafy branches of a large oak tree. He was spreading out the blanket she'd brought with them when she saw Sawyer and Asher coming down the walk.

For a second Lia thought about not saying anything and hoping they didn't see her or Shane. Ever since Sawyer had found out she was carrying Shane's baby, he'd gone from being warm and friendly to all business.

Asher, whom she'd only seen from a distance a few times, held the hand of a small boy who looked about four or five. His son? Probably.

The child looked like his dad with dirty-blond hair and blue eyes. Those blue eyes reminded her of Shane's and Lia couldn't help wondering if her baby would look like him.

The men drew closer and instead of looking away, Lia nudged Shane. "Your brothers are here."

Shane straightened and turned. Though a smile lifted his lips and he called out a greeting, he looked more annoyed than pleased.

"What have we here?" Sawyer's gaze met hers. The suspicion and coolness to his blue eyes made her shiver.

"Hi, Sawyer." Lia forced a friendliness to her voice that up until a few days ago would have been second nature. She shifted her gaze to the father and son and widened her smile.

Shane slipped an arm around her shoulders and the phony smile froze on Sawyer's lips. "I know you've met Sawyer, but these two with him are my brother Asher and my nephew Jace. Asher, this is Natalia Serrano."

"Pleased to meet you, Asher," Lia said, shaking his hand.

There was a touch of sympathy in Asher's eyes that she didn't expect. "Nice to finally meet you, Ms. Serrano."

"Please," she said. "Call me Lia."

She crouched down until she was at eye level with the small boy. "Hi, Jace. My name is Lia. Are you having fun?"

The little boy smiled. "My daddy is going to get me a tamale."

"That's nice of him. I love tamales."

The little boy considered her words for several seconds. "Maybe my daddy will get you one, too."

Lia simply smiled and ruffled his hair. "Your uncle Shane has promised me dinner tonight. I think I'm going to ask for tamales."

"You're pretty," Jace said.

"Thank you, Jace," Lia said.

"Well," said Asher, shooting Shane an apologetic smile, "we should keep moving. We'll touch base tomorrow?"

A look passed between the three men and Shane nodded.

"Do you have a big business deal in the works?" Lia asked once his brothers and nephew were out of earshot.

"Nope. Just some family business," Shane said with an easy smile then changed the subject to dinner.

It turned out Shane liked tamales as much as she did, and he was soon heading off to get some before the vendor ran out.

Lia waited for him to return, mindful of all the curious glances being slanted in her direction. In Red Rock, the Fortune family, especially the four handsome brothers, were celebrities.

"I wasn't sure if tamales would be enough." Shane's return pulled Lia from her reverie. "So I got us a little bit of everything."

He sat down and began pulling tamales and churros, corn dogs and hamburgers out of various paper bags.

"They all look good," she said diplomatically, resisting the urge to calculate in her head how much money he'd spent. "I don't know how to pick."

He considered the food spread out before them. "We could share. Have some of each."

"Sounds like a stellar solution."

They ended up evaluating each item as if they were food critics. By the time they finished, Lia was stuffed and had laughed more than she had in months.

Shane rested his back against the tree and motioned to her. "Come over here."

Lia hesitated for only a second before she scooted between his legs and rested her back against his broad chest. He wrapped his arms lightly around her and she relaxed against him.

The bluesy jazz tune soon began to sound like a lullaby. Her lids grew heavy and she let them drift shut for a second. She wasn't sure how long she slept. All she knew was she was startled awake by a clap of thunder.

Shane brushed a strand of hair from her face when she looked up at him. "Storm is moving in. We'd better start walking back."

Lia hurriedly gathered up the blanket while Shane dumped the trash. Another loud crack split the air and a few fat raindrops fell on her hair.

Those around them seemed to realize at exactly the same time that if they didn't hustle, they were going to get wet. Lia worried she and Shane might get separated in the jostling crowd, but he kept a firm grip on her arm.

By the time they reached her block, drops splattered the dusty sidewalk in increasing numbers. Shane pulled her into the doorway of her building as sheets of rain swept over the street.

Lia lifted her gaze to Shane. "Come up for a few minutes. You shouldn't drive in this weather."

He smiled. "Offer accepted."

They stepped inside just as hail began battering the roof of the building. She turned to him with a worried frown. "I hope your car won't get damaged."

"It's a rental." Shane waved a dismissive hand. "I'm just thankful you didn't get too wet."

"Maybe my luck is changing," she quipped.

He stared at her for a long moment but didn't say anything more as they climbed the stairs to her floor.

Lia unlocked the door, stepped inside and gestured for him to take a seat on a well-worn sofa in a woven Southwestern plaid. "It's a little late for coffee and I don't have any alcohol, but I could make us some cocoa?"

He opened his mouth and for a second she thought he was going to decline her offer. Then he smiled. "Sounds good."

Warmth spread like honey to fill every inch of Lia's body. The response to a simple smile reminded her why she'd gone to bed with Shane that long-ago night. She had felt a connection to him, a bond that seemed to transcend the physical. Lia couldn't explain it. All she knew was that tie between them was still there.

Her phone rang just as she placed two steaming mugs of hot cocoa on the coffee table and took a seat beside him. She pulled the phone from her pocket and glanced at the screen. Stephanie Roberts. She let it go to voice mail.

"You can take that call if you want."

"It's just a girlfriend wanting to make lunch plans." She nudged his mug closer to him. "I hope you like marshmallows."

Okay, so maybe she'd gone a little crazy with the marshmallows, but as far as Lia was concerned, they were the best part.

His gaze traveled slowly down her body, never once glancing in the direction of the mug. "Looks delicious."

Despite the shiver of awareness that rippled across her skin, Lia reminded herself she was pregnant. Hardly a woman to inspire lascivious thoughts. She must have confused the yearning in his eyes with her own desire.

"Do you want to watch television?" She gestured to her ancient set.

"I've got a better idea."

She was almost afraid to ask. "What is that?"

"You can tell me about you, give me the inside scoop on what makes Lia Serrano tick." He smiled engagingly. "I'd like to get to know you better."

Lia thought for a moment. It wasn't that she didn't think what he was suggesting was a good idea. Since she would be the mother of his child, she did want him to get to know her.

But she also wanted to get to know *him*. Because they were in this together.

"I've an even better idea." She rose, waving away his protests. "I'll be right back."

She returned less than a minute later with a deck of cards.

A look of dismay crossed his face. "You want to play cards?"

Lia smiled and plopped down on the sofa next to him. "Not in the way you're thinking. This is a deck of getting-to-know-you cards. The game is called Heart-to-Heart. I got it for a birthday present several years ago from one of my friends." She expertly shuffled the deck. "There's a different question on each card. When the card has two hearts on it, both of us have to answer the question. Otherwise we simply take turns drawing, and whatever question is on the card we draw, we have to answer."

Shane took a sip of hot cocoa. From the doubtful expression on his face, this obviously wasn't what he'd had in mind.

"Do you want to draw or should I go first?" She held out the deck, not giving him the option of saying no.

"You first," he said, just as she expected.

She pulled a card from the top of the deck.

"Read it aloud," he said.

"'What music do you and your father have in common?'" A familiar sense of longing for something she'd never known gripped her heart. She glanced at Shane.

"Your game. Your rules," he reminded her. "You have to answer."

She lifted a shoulder in a helpless shrug. "I barely remember my father."

Shane's gaze searched hers. "What happened to him?"

"He left when I was three. I have memories of him laughing and tossing me up in the air, but I'm not sure they're real or just stories." Lia waited for Shane to say something but he simply took another sip of his drink and gazed at her with an expectant expression.

Of course he wouldn't give her a pass. If Lia was in his position, she wouldn't, either. You didn't get to know someone by skirting around difficult issues. "He'd just turned thirty. One day he informed my mother he was leaving. Told her the life he had wasn't the one he wanted."

Lia picked at a loose thread on the sofa upholstery, wondering how she could feel such a loss over a man she barely remembered. "We never saw him again."

Shane swore under his breath. "How did you survive?"

"My grandparents were very supportive. My mother worked two jobs, and as soon as my brother and I were old enough, we were expected to work and help out."

"Has he tried to contact you?"

Lia shook her head.

"I can only imagine how you feel about him," Shane mused. "You must despise the man."

"Actually, I feel sorry for him." Lia smiled at Shane's look of startled surprise. "He ultimately came out the loser."

"He missed seeing you grow up."

"And my brother." Lia wrapped her fingers around the mug, finding comfort in the warmth. "Big loss."

She wondered if Shane saw the similarity with their situation. Would he walk away from *his* child and live to regret it?

Several heartbeats of silence passed between them before Lia gestured to the deck. "Your turn."

With a resigned look, Shane moved the top half of the deck aside and selected a card from the middle.

"Read the question," Lia urged. "Aloud."

His eyes scanned the words on the card. "'Do you think "honesty is the best policy"? Why or why not?'"

"That should be an easy one." Lia wondered why he was even hesitating.

"On the whole, I believe honesty is the best policy," Shane said slowly. "But if telling the truth might hurt someone, then it might be better to lie."

She understood where he was coming from, but she couldn't sit silently and have him think she agreed. "But the person you mislead is eventually going to find out that you lied and then, not only would they be hurt, but it'd be hard for them to trust you again."

Shane stared at her for a long moment and a look she couldn't quite decipher filled his eyes. "If I'm hearing you right, you believe honesty is always the best policy."

"This isn't my question," she gently reminded him.

"Yes, but I assume these questions are intended to stimulate discussion."

Lia thought for a moment then nodded.

"That's what we're having," Shane said. "A discussion."

"Then, yes, I would say that I believe honesty is always the best policy." Lia punctuated her comment with a decisive nod.

"Interesting," Shane said, an enigmatic look on his face.

"Why interesting?"

"No reason." His gaze grew thoughtful. "I like this game."

"I knew if you gave it a chance you would."

He smiled. "And you're always right."

She nodded, returning his smile. "Pretty much."

"Your turn."

She pulled out a card. She held it up for him to see. "This one has two hearts so it's for both of us."

"This game is rigged," he muttered.

Lia smiled. He liked the game all right, as long as she was the one answering the questions. She read the question aloud. "'What goals do you have for your children?'"

"It does not ask that."

She held up the card. "See for yourself."

"Okay," he said finally. "But you drew it, so you answer first."

The question struck at the heart of her fears for this child she carried. "I want her to be a happy, well-adjusted child."

Shane raised a brow. *"Her?"*

"Dr. Gray thinks the baby is a girl. When she did the ultrasound, we didn't see any, uh, hanging appendages. But then we didn't have any really good views, either."

"Why didn't you tell me?"

"I thought if you were interested, you'd ask."

For a long moment neither of them spoke.

"What are your goals for her?" he asked.

"I told you." For someone who appeared to be giving her his full attention, he seemed to miss about half of what she said. "I want her to grow up to be happy and well-adjusted, to find her passion in life."

"And?" he prompted.

"What do you mean?"

"What about education?"

"I want her to get the most out of her classroom experiences, and as much as I'm able, I want to give her good life lessons." Lia glanced at him. "What about you? What goals do you have for your child?"

"The same as yours," he said, quickly picking up the deck, his blue eyes giving nothing away.

Lia considered challenging the lukewarm response, but decided to let it go. If Shane Fortune didn't want to answer, she wasn't going to pry it out of him.

She lifted a brow. "Are you going to just hold the cards, or draw one?"

With an exaggerated sigh, he pulled a card. His eyes darkened. His lips pressed together.

"What does it ask?" she prompted.

"'Who do you think you are most like in your family?'" he read.

"That's an interesting question," Lia observed. "Who is it for you?"

"My father." Shane spat the word as if it was bitter on his tongue. "We're driven in the same way about business. We have the same management style, though he can be a bully at times. In other ways, we're not alike at all."

Lia could feel the conflicting emotions bubbling up inside him. It was obvious Shane didn't want to be like his father. But why? From what she'd read, James Marshall Fortune was the successful founder of JMF Financial, married for many years to his wife, Clara. Father of four boys and one girl.

"Was he a good father?" she asked in an offhand tone as if it didn't matter if he answered or not. The truth was, she wanted to know what kind of role model Shane had experienced growing up.

"He was," Shane admitted, almost grudgingly. "Though he was always busy with work, he took time for us. Dad is very athletic and, consequently, all of us kids were active in sports when we were young. Our vacations were always centered around activities like white-water rafting, skiing, hiking."

"Sounds like fun," Lia said wistfully, thinking of her brothers and how much they'd missed by having an absent father.

"It was." Shane's lips curved up in a slight smile before the mask descended again. "But times change. People change."

"Do you really believe that?" Lia took another sip of cocoa, pondering the thought.

"Your ex-boyfriend changed."

"Did he? Or was it that I saw in him only what I wanted to see?" She shook her head. "It's so easy to be fooled and to think someone is different than they really are."

Shane's gaze traveled over her. "Are you saying he fooled you?"

"Maybe." She shrugged. "Or perhaps I only saw the good and didn't pay enough attention to the bad. If I ever get involved in another relationship, I won't be willing to take a man at face value."

"What do you mean 'if' you ever get involved? How old are you? Early twenties?"

"I'm twenty-five."

"You're too young to be giving up on men."

"You forget. I'll soon have a child to raise. She'll be my priority." Lia waited, though she wasn't exactly certain just what she wanted him to say.

Perhaps that he would be there to help. Or that she really wasn't in this alone, because she had him. But he didn't say anything like that, which, given his ambivalence, might be for the best anyway. Because they'd be empty words.

"But what if the perfect man happened to drop right in your lap?"

"I'd be instantly suspicious."

He grinned unexpectedly. "Why?"

"Because there are no perfect men."

"Only perfect women?" he teased.

She smiled and shook her head. "I doubt there are any of those out there, either."

"But what if a good man, or someone who appeared to

be a good man, came into your life? Are you saying you wouldn't give him a chance?"

"I'm not saying that at all." She met his gaze. "I'm just saying that when you're assessing anyone's character, you have to keep your eyes wide open. And to always remember that actions speak louder than words."

## Chapter Nine

"Do you recall the time Dad took us white-water rafting down the Colorado River?" Shane asked his brother Sawyer over lunch at Red.

Sawyer looked up from his burrito. Unexpectedly he grinned. "How could I forget? We went something like two hundred kilometers in six days. It was crazy."

"Yeah." Shane glanced down at his food, remembering all the fun they'd had sleeping in tents and eating food they'd cooked over an open fire. "Crazy."

His brother's tone grew curious. "What made you think of that trip?"

Shane shrugged but met his brother's gaze. "I've been trying to figure out just when Dad changed. And how we didn't notice."

Sawyer had been as disturbed as Shane by the notion that their father might have had another family squirreled away all these years. "The thing I can't figure out is when he had the time."

"You and I both know how busy he's always been. When he did have free time, he was doing stuff with us or taking Mom on some kind of trip." Shane wasn't sure what had brought up this sudden need to revisit his father's guilt, but the pieces didn't all fit.

"Unless," Sawyer said slowly, "those business trips weren't business trips. He might have used some of that time to see her."

Shane reluctantly conceded that could be the case. "It's possible."

"What got you thinking of this again? I thought we'd talked this subject into the ground."

"Lia."

Sawyer's eyes widened. He dropped his fork to his plate. "You told her about Dad?"

"Of course not," Shane snapped. "We were playing this card game and the subject of trust, or something like that, came up."

"What card game was that?"

"A girlie one."

"I can't believe you agreed to play."

"I thought it would be a way to get to know her better."

"Did it work?"

Shane took a sip of cola and grudgingly nodded. "It's still too early for any conclusions."

"Has the attorney heard anything from the detective?"

"Not yet. I should get a report in the next day or two." Shane wondered what Lia would think if she discovered he had a detective snooping into her background.

"I'd like to fire her," Sawyer said in a matter-of-fact tone. "Every time I think how she's trying to shake you down, it makes me angry."

"Don't fire her," Shane said immediately. "You need the help."

"Not that badly." A hard look filled Sawyer's eyes. "I can find someone else."

"I'm telling you, don't do anything, Sawyer." Shane's tone brooked no argument. "Lia needs the money you're paying her to survive."

Sawyer narrowed his gaze. "You sound as if you care for her."

Shane kept his face expressionless. "She might be carrying my baby."

"From what you've said, the odds are she's not."

"But if she is, I want her to be able to take care of herself." Shane paused. He was still considering another option and hadn't planned on mentioning his thoughts to his brother yet. But they were alone and this was probably as good a time as any. "I'm thinking of asking her to stay at New Fortunes Ranch for the rest of her pregnancy."

"Are you nuts?" Sawyer's voice rose, but he paused when Shane shot him a quelling glance. "Why would you do that?"

"We have room."

"That's not the point. It's like asking a thief to move in with you and, hey, while you're at it, giving her the combination to the safe."

"Lia is not a thief." Shane's voice held a steely edge.

"She's trying to force a baby on you that isn't yours."

"We don't know that for sure." Shane pointed out, "The fact is she may be carrying my baby. On the off chance that she is, I don't want her living in that hovel downtown. That area isn't safe, especially not for a woman living alone."

Sawyer's jaw lifted in a stubborn tilt. "I don't like where this is going."

"Think about what the attorney said. We need to keep her close. We need to find out her weaknesses so we can exploit them. If that baby girl is mine and she tries to fight for custody, we'll need that information."

"That part makes sense," Sawyer said grudgingly then paused and cocked his head. "She's having a girl?"

"That's what the doctor thinks, but wasn't willing to say for sure." Shane had to admit when he'd heard the baby was a girl, he'd found himself wondering what it would look like if it were his child. Dark hair for sure. But would she have his blue eyes? Or Lia's beautiful chocolate-brown ones? He shook the image from his brain. "I'm going to ask her tonight to move in. I'll let you know what she says."

Sawyer made a scoffing sound. "Of course she'll say yes. Turn down a chance to live at the ranch for a dump on Main Street? A woman would have to be crazy to say no."


"No." Lia looked up from her computer screen and met Shane's gaze. "Thank you for the offer, but I'm not interested."

"I don't understand," Shane said. "You'd have a big, beautiful room here. The adjoining bathroom even has one of those rain showerheads you liked so much in the hotel room. Think of the rent money you'd save. Think of how nice it'd be to not have to drive back and forth to work. A few steps out the front door and you'd be in your office."

Lia saved the entries she'd just made on the spreadsheet and gave Shane her full attention. He'd surprised her by unexpectedly showing up this afternoon. She thought he'd simply wanted to say hello. Then he'd asked her to move into the ranch house.

"Thank you for thinking of me. It's a generous offer. And I know it would be nice." She spoke slowly and deliberately. While she wanted him to know she appreciated the offer, there was no way she was going to agree. "At this time, I think it's important for me to have my own place."

"Are you still going to live in that dump after the baby is born? What if the test determines the child is mine? Are you still going to refuse my help?"

"The baby is yours, Shane." Lia rubbed the bridge of her nose with her fingers. "And we'll deal with the issue of your support once you accept that fact."

Out of the corner of her eye, Lia saw Sawyer going through a file cabinet in the other room. From where he stood, she knew he could hear every word being said. She stood and retrieved a small canvas tote from under the desk. "Let me change my shoes. We'll go for a walk."

"We haven't finished our discussion."

"That's what we'll do on the walk." Lia slipped off her pumps and quickly put on a pair of lightweight bamboo socks and a pair of red canvas shoes.

"That's quite a fashion statement." Shane's lips quirked upward as he gazed at her bright-yellow-and-white-striped dress with the red shoes.

"I have my own style lately, that's for sure," Lia muttered.

"I'm glad to see you're not taking any unnecessary risks."

Lia lifted a brow. "Risks?"

"Of falling." He glanced pointedly at the heels she was stuffing into the canvas bag.

There appeared to be genuine concern in his eyes. Just like the other night over hot cocoa, the sense of camaraderie she'd experienced with him on New Year's Eve returned.

But instead of reassuring her, Lia worried. She'd been serious when she'd told Shane that she was going to be careful who she trusted in the future.

She'd always thought of herself as a strong woman, but lately she'd begun to worry she might be weak.

She'd wanted a degree in fine arts, yet she'd let her brother Eric talk her into a degree in business.

She'd felt twinges of concern during her relationship with David, yet she'd ignored them. Why? Had it been simply easier to believe his excuses on why he was spending so much time in San Antonio?

Shane…well, he confused her. Sometimes she had the feeling he genuinely cared. Other times, she got the impression he was playing some kind of game that only he understood.

With her daughter's—or son's—life and happiness at stake, she must proceed with caution.

Shane held open the door and they stepped from the cool air-conditioned building into the warmth of the day.

"Wow, it's hotter out here than I realized." Thankfully a large cypress tree bore the brunt of the bright sun.

Shane held out his arm. "We'll talk in the house. No one will disturb us there."

She took his arm. "That would be nice."

"Do you have dinner plans this evening?" he asked conversationally on their way to the sprawling ranch house.

"Some friends and I are getting together at one of the bars downtown. They have free appetizers on Wednesday night and half-price drinks."

"Sounds like fun."

"Do you want to come?" The second the invitation popped out of Lia's mouth, she wished she could call it back.

"I don't think—" he began and she released the breath she'd been holding.

"That's okay," she said quickly. "It's not your kind of place anyway."

He lifted a brow, suddenly looking intrigued. "My kind of place?"

"It's not fancy," she said, sending up a mental apology to the owners of Pappacito's for what she was about to say. "In fact, it's kind of a dive. But a nice dive. Definitely not the Red Rock Country Club."

"But you like it." His blue eyes glittered in the sunlight. "And you go there…frequently?"

She nodded then shrugged. "They have great food. But it can be noisy and crowded."

"Not the place to discuss why you won't move into the ranch house."

Lia shook off the rest of her unease. "Definitely not."

Shane smiled. "Then we'll discuss it now, so tonight we can just have fun."

When they reached the steps of the house, he opened the door and motioned her inside. If they had more time he'd have given her a tour, but she was still on the clock and would want to get back to work before long. Shane ushered her into the kitchen and got them each a glass of lemonade.

The house was cool and quiet, the lemonade ice-cold. They sat across from each other at the small white table in an alcove off the kitchen.

"It's pretty in here." Her gaze lingered on the yellow gingham place mats and the riotous bouquet of wildflowers spilling from a copper coffeepot in the middle of the table.

"It's comfortable." She'd given him an opening and Shane was going to run with it. "You'd like it here."

"I'm sure I would." Lia took a long drink and set the tumbler on the table. "That's not the issue."

He merely cocked his head.

"I have a place to live—"

She stopped, frowned at the derisive snort that had escaped before he could stop it.

"Let me finish." This time when she spoke her tone was

cool. "As I was saying, I have a place to live. And, as long as I pay my rent, it's mine."

Though Shane wanted to point out she wouldn't have any rent if she moved in here, something in her eyes told him to remain silent. He offered an encouraging smile.

"From the time I've been old enough to work, I've made my own way. I'm a strong person." She lifted her chin and met his gaze, as if daring him to say differently. "I'm not some damsel in distress who needs a man to rescue her."

"You are strong," Shane said honestly. "Still, there's no reason you have to do this alone. I want to make things easier for you."

She raked a hand through her hair and there was weariness in the gesture. "I can handle it."

Shane told himself to let it go. He'd offered. She'd given him her decision. But she mattered to him…in a way he didn't fully understand. Reaching across the table, he grasped her hands with a sense of urgency. "Let me help."

He expected her to pull away. Instead she gazed down at their joined hands. When she looked up, a smile lifted her lips. "You have already."

Baffled, he could only stare.

"Just by being here," she told him, giving his hands a squeeze. "And letting me know you care."

Shane must have passed the small café and bar on Sycamore Street many times before, but it hadn't made enough of an impression to warrant him remembering it.

The sign on the front of the building was in need of painting and the frontage was small and nondescript. When he opened the front door and Lia stepped inside, the combination of the noise from a mariachi band and the din of conversation assaulted his senses.

A long U-shaped bar was to the left. Though it was

still early, every stool around the highly polished bar was filled. Patrons who hadn't been lucky enough to get a seat milled around with drinks in their hands.

Lia stood on her tiptoes and glanced around the area, looking for her friends.

In her multicolored skirt and bright green shirt she looked ready to party. She'd pulled her hair back from her face with two clips adorned with brightly colored stones. Bright red hoops dangled from her ears.

When he'd stopped by her apartment to pick her up and she'd said it was close enough to walk, he'd taken one look at her shoes and shaken his head.

The green wedge sandals had to be at least three inches high. But she'd waved away his concerns, telling him if she got tired of walking, they could get a cab.

Surprisingly, she hadn't experienced any difficulty until they were almost at the café, when she'd tripped on an uneven piece of concrete.

She'd lurched forward but his hand had been there to steady her. When she'd smiled her thanks, he'd experienced an almost overpowering urge to pull her close and kiss her.

He experienced that same urge now.

"Perhaps they were lucky and got a table." Without another word she started toward the back of the bar, leaving him to follow.

On the way to Pappacito's, Lia had informed him they were meeting her friends Selina and Doriann, whom everyone called Dori. There would be another guy there, as well—Dori's on-again, off-again boyfriend, Jax.

Shane had a pile of work on his desk but when Lia had invited him to go out with her friends to a place that "wasn't very nice," he couldn't pass up the opportunity.

Hadn't someone once said you could be judged by the

company you kept? And who knew when he'd have another chance to meet her friends?

At least that was why Shane told himself he was here. To continue to gather information that might come in handy later. It didn't have a thing to do with wanting to spend time with Lia.

"There they are." Lia's voice rose. A big smile crossed her face. She waved wildly.

The three sat around a table for four, bottles of Corona in front of them, along with a huge plate of nachos. Shane could tell by the looks on their faces they were shocked. He assumed it was because she'd brought a "date."

"Natalia, you look radiant," a thin woman with masses of dark curly hair said in lieu of a proper greeting. "But I'd never guess you were pregnant if Selina hadn't told me."

By the process of elimination Shane figured she must be Dori and the other woman Selina. "You're pregnant?" Jax glanced at Dori. "Nobody tells me anything."

"Who's this with you?" Selina asked in a sultry voice, gazing at Shane through lowered lashes.

"This is my friend Shane," Lia said carelessly and Shane wasn't sure if her omission of his last name was deliberate or accidental.

Lia went to grab a chair from a nearby table but Shane took it from her hands then waited for her to take a seat before he sat. She quickly performed the introductions.

"Where have you been keeping him?" Selina asked Lia.

When she hesitated, Shane smiled. "I've been out of town since the first of the year."

"Oh." Selina raised a brow. "Doing what?"

"Working," Lia said before he could answer. "Now, will you quit interrogating him and tell me what's been going on with you guys? It seems like forever since we've talked."

While the server brought Lia a virgin margarita and him a beer, Lia's friends updated her on their activities over the past few months. From how far back they went, it was obvious it had been quite some time since Lia had seen them.

"The last time Natalia and I really went out was New Year's Eve," Selina told Jax. "Isn't that unbelievable?"

"The party at the hotel." A dreamy look filled Dori's eyes. "Jax and I had the best time. We danced and drank too much... It was one of the best New Year's Eves ever."

Jax nodded his agreement and leaned back in his seat, seemingly content to let the women talk.

Shane decided it was a good strategy to follow.

"It was fun, until *mi amiga* decided to ditch me." Selina slanted a speculative gaze in Shane's direction. "You wouldn't have had anything to do with her disappearance, would you?"

"Selina, you were so into Jorge that night that you didn't know if I was there or not." Lia's tone started out serious but quickly turned teasing. "We both know you bailed on me."

"What can I say?" Selina's lips curved up in a Cheshire cat smile. "Men see me. They want me. It's a curse."

Shane took a sip of beer and glanced at the menu.

"They have the best chiles rellenos." Lia leaned close to share her menu. The familiar scent of Chanel teased his nostrils. "Would you split an order with me?"

"Sure." Shane wasn't really here to eat—more to observe—but the smells in the air made him hungry. For food. For her.

Conversation flowed easily around the table, with topics ranging from sports—they were all San Antonio Spurs fans—to the economy.

Apparently Jax had been recently laid off from his job as a programmer.

# ♦HARLEQUIN® READER SERVICE—Here's How It Works:

Accepting your 2 free books and 2 free gifts (gifts valued at approximately $10.00) places you under no obligation to buy anything. You may keep the books and gifts and return the shipping statement marked "cancel". If you do not cancel, about a month later we'll send you 6 additional books and bill you just $4.74 each in the U.S. or $5.24 each in Canada. That's a savings of at least 14% off the cover price. It's quite a bargain! Shipping and handling is just 50¢ per book in the U.S. and 75¢ per book in Canada.* You may cancel at any time, but if you choose to continue, every month we'll send you 6 more books, which you may either purchase at the discount price or return to us and cancel your subscription.

*Terms and prices subject to change without notice. Prices do not include applicable taxes. Sales tax applicable in N.Y. Canadian residents will be charged applicable taxes. Offer not valid in Quebec. All orders subject to credit approval. Credit or debit balances in a customer's account(s) may be offset by any other outstanding balance owed by or to the customer. Please allow 4 to 6 weeks for delivery. Offer available while quantities last.

If offer card is missing write to: Harlequin Reader Service, P.O. Box 1867, Buffalo NY 14240-1867 or visit www.ReaderService.com

HSE-L7-05/13

NO POSTAGE
NECESSARY
IF MAILED
IN THE
UNITED STATES

## BUSINESS REPLY MAIL
FIRST-CLASS MAIL    PERMIT NO. 717    BUFFALO, NY

POSTAGE WILL BE PAID BY ADDRESSEE

**HARLEQUIN READER SERVICE**
PO BOX 1867
BUFFALO NY 14240-9952

# GET FREE BOOKS and FREE GIFTS WHEN YOU PLAY THE...

**Lucky 7**

*Just scratch off the silver box with a coin. Then check below to see the gifts you get!*

## SLOT MACHINE GAME!

# YES! I have scratched off the silver box. Please send me the 2 free Harlequin® Special Edition® books and 2 free gifts for which I qualify. I understand I am under no obligation to purchase any books, as explained on the back of this card.

### 235/335 HDL FV7W

FIRST NAME

LAST NAME

ADDRESS

APT.#

CITY

STATE/PROV.

ZIP/POSTAL CODE

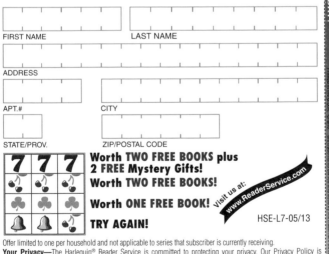

Worth TWO FREE BOOKS plus 2 FREE Mystery Gifts!

Worth TWO FREE BOOKS!

Worth ONE FREE BOOK!

TRY AGAIN!

Visit us at: www.ReaderService.com

HSE-L7-05/13

Printed in the U.S.A. ® and ™ are trademarks owned and used by the trademark owner and/or its licensee.

© 2012 HARLEQUIN ENTERPRISES LIMITED

HSE-L7-05/13

"You'll find another job," Lia said encouragingly. "And it will be better than the last one. Look at me. I like the job I have now so much more than the one I lost."

"That's what I told him," Dori said. "And if he can't find something here, there are lots of jobs in San Antonio."

"What do you do, Shane?" Selina asked.

Lia opened her mouth but Shane refused to have her answer for him again.

"Right now I'm involved with a family business, but I'm contemplating making a change." Leaving JMF Financial wouldn't be easy, not after all the work he'd put into the company. But if it came down to working with his dad's mistress, he'd walk away in a heartbeat.

"Is your current job stable?" Jax asked.

Shane nodded.

"I'd think long and hard about making a move in to-day's economy," Jax warned. Selina and Dori nodded their agreement. "Ask Natalia how scary it can be without any money coming in."

"I did okay." Lia shifted uncomfortably in her seat. "I had my beading money to tide me over."

"You ate at the Kitchen," Selina reminded her.

"Just once."

Dori pinned Lia with her gaze.

"Okay," Lia admitted. "Maybe three times."

"The Kitchen?" Shane asked, an uneasy feeling in the pit of his stomach.

"The Red Rock Kitchen," Jax explained. "It's not far from here. It's a hunger-relief program. They serve two hot meals daily to the destitute."

Shane settled his gaze on Lia, more disturbed than he was letting on. "You had to go to The Red Rock Kitchen so you could eat?"

Lia lifted her chin. "I've volunteered there for years.

Pastor Tom—he's in charge of the operation—said there's no shame in accepting help when you need it."

The conversation was cut short when the waiter brought out the food. The deep-fried chili peppers stuffed with cheese were huge. He could see why Lia thought she couldn't handle a full order. But even though her share was small, she barely touched the food. It was as if the discussion about the hunger-relief program had stolen her appetite.

The truth was, visualizing the proud young woman sitting beside him standing in line for free food had stolen his appetite, as well. It was difficult for him to wrap his mind around the thought.

The woman who might be carrying his child had been in the position of relying on the generosity of strangers in order to have enough to eat. The realization left a bitter taste in his mouth.

Lia deserved better. And he was going to see that she got it.

## Chapter Ten

Never in her wildest dreams had Lia thought she'd be spending Saturday afternoon serving lunch to the needy with Shane Fortune. She glanced to her side and realized, even dressed very casually in jeans and a polo shirt, he stood out.

He had left his expensive watch at home but everything from his haircut to his leather loafers screamed, *I have money.*

But she had to admit, he'd been amazingly kind and solicitous to the people who'd come to The Red Rock Kitchen for a hot meal. He was dishing up whipped potatoes while she was in charge of the creamed corn.

The cavernous hall had the AC blasting and large commercial fans but Lia was still hot.

"Are you okay?" Shane asked, his concerned gaze focused on the droplets of sweat on her face.

"It's a little warm in here." She wiped the perspiration off onto her sleeve.

"Cooler in here than it is out there," a man going through the line commented.

"You're right." Lia gave the man, a biker dude wearing a blue bandanna, a warm smile. "It's good to be out of the sun."

"Going to be another hot one today." An older woman, in line behind the man, held out her plate. She wore a thin gray housedress that appeared to have once been a bright blue.

Lia added a large spoonful of creamed corn to her plate and realized they'd reached the end of the line.

"That's it for today," the pastor told the volunteers. "There's enough food here for all of you, so we hope you'll stay and socialize."

Pastor Tom was in his early fifties with wiry gray hair and a smile that never seemed to leave his lips. He had abundant energy and a passion for ministering to those in need.

When Lia had told him that Shane wanted to volunteer with her today, he'd welcomed him warmly, but hadn't fawned over him because of his family connections.

"Where do you want to go for lunch?" Shane asked.

Lia looked at him in surprise. "I thought we'd eat here."

"You're hot. I thought you'd want to go someplace where you could relax."

"All the volunteers stay and eat," Lia said slowly. "It's a way of saying to the people who come here that we're all one. I'm probably not explaining it well but…"

"You're doing a good job. I understand." He took her hand then laughed as he realized they both had on the plastic gloves. He gently stripped hers off her hands. "Turkey. Whipped potatoes. Who could ask for more?"

"Don't forget the creamed corn."

"I could never forget that," he said teasingly as they went to get their plates and rolled-up silverware.

By the time they sat down and got their glasses of iced tea, Lia's dress was plastered to her back. But the table where they sat got a good breeze from the fan and she quickly cooled off.

It wasn't long until Pastor Tom, who'd been making his way around the room with a tall glass of iced tea in one hand, stopped at their table and took a seat. "How did you like volunteering, Mr. Fortune?"

"Please call me Shane."

"Okay, Shane. Was it how you thought it would be?"

"I'd say it was an eye-opening experience." Shane idly stabbed a piece of turkey but didn't raise his fork. "It made me realize just how many people in Red Rock are struggling."

"This is a prosperous community." Pastor Tom's expression turned serious. "But we also have many who fit the definition of the *working poor*. They barely get by. If one thing goes wrong, it can send them into a tailspin. They simply don't have the resources to weather a crisis."

"Like losing a job," Lia added.

Pastor Tom nodded but didn't say anything more. He didn't gossip about the people who came for services.

"I told Shane that I came here several times after I lost my job," Lia said to the pastor then shifted her gaze to Shane. "Pastor Tom helped me see things in a new light. It was very profound."

"I remember a discussion." Pastor Tom took a long sip of tea. "But not anything particularly profound."

Curiosity filled Shane's blue eyes. "What did he say that you found so insightful?"

"He told me that by not availing myself of the services offered here when I needed them, I was saying to those who did come here that they shouldn't, either." Lia smiled at Pastor Tom. "Using the services also gave me a greater appreciation for how hard it is for people to walk through those doors the first time. Now I really go out of my way to make everyone, especially the first-timers, feel welcome."

"It's often through adversity that we learn our greatest lessons." The pastor patted Lia's hand. "How you've dealt with this latest challenge in your life shows me you're made of strong stuff. You'll do just fine."

"Pastor Tom." A tall, thin woman wearing a stained white apron appeared in the doorway to the kitchen. "The dishwasher is on the fritz again."

"Just needs a good strong whack on the side." Pastor Tom grinned. "Luckily, I have the magic touch."

He rose to his feet and Shane stood, as well.

"You've got a great operation here, Pastor." Shane glanced around, his eyes thoughtful. "You're doing a lot of good for a lot of people."

"If everyone gives a little, we gain a lot. Thanks for helping today. We always need volunteers." The pastor's gaze slid to Lia. "See you next Saturday?"

"Count on it," she said with a smile.

"I mean it—you're welcome anytime." The pastor took Shane's hand, cupping it between his. "God bless you."

After Pastor Tom left for the kitchen, Shane sat down in the chair next to Lia and shook his head. "I had no idea any of this existed in Red Rock."

"Cut yourself some slack." Lia appeared more amused than condemning. "You're new to the community. And this isn't exactly your social circle."

"You work all week and then volunteer here on Saturdays?"

He made it sound as if she did so much, when in fact she felt as if she was doing the bare minimum.

"I enjoy it." Lia speared a piece of turkey with her fork and brought it to her lips. "Didn't it make you feel good to help someone else?"

"It made me feel as if I'm not doing enough to help."

"That's the way it should be." Lia smiled. "We should always challenge ourselves to do more, to give more."

"You're an amazing woman, Natalia Serrano."

Lia brushed a damp strand of hair back from her cheek and shot him an impish smile. "Don't tell me you're just figuring that out?"

The large table positioned next to the wall of windows overlooking the golf course afforded the diners a good view of the deepening twilight.

When Shane had learned his brothers were bringing their significant others, he'd asked Lia to join his family for dinner Tuesday night at the country club. Not that Lia was his significant other.

He had to keep reminding himself that she could be a grifter playing a really good con. But if all she wanted was to pin this baby on someone, why didn't she simply tell her ex it was his?

Granted, from what she'd told him, it was apparent the car salesman didn't have either money or position. Yet Lia had to know any Fortune facing this situation would demand a paternity test, while Doug would probably take her word. It just didn't add up.

She laughed at something Wyatt said and Shane shifted his gaze to her. With her butterscotch-colored skin tone and all that long, dark hair, from his perspective there wasn't a more beautiful woman in the room. The short-sleeved red dress she had on today left no doubt that she was expecting. The stretchy fabric clung to her ever-increasing midsection and even the brightly colored stones around the neckline weren't enough to draw his attention from her belly.

Lia had quickly established a rapport with Marnie Mc-Cafferty, who'd come with Asher and Jace. A riding instructor and former nanny, Marnie had made his brother believe there could be happiness after a bitter divorce. The two had recently announced their engagement.

Sarah-Jane Early, his brother Wyatt's fiancée, was the assistant manager of The Stocking Stitch, a local yarn and knitting store. Shane couldn't remember the last time he'd seen his brother so happy.

"What's this I hear about you serving in some soup kitchen?" Sawyer asked, his gaze focused on Shane.

"I read about it in the newspaper," Sarah-Jane piped up. "There was a picture of you and Lia."

Lia's grimace told him she'd seen the photo. "I shouldn't have pulled my hair back in a ponytail. It doesn't translate well in pictures."

"You looked darling." Marnie leaned over and placed a reassuring hand on Lia's arm. "Supercute."

"Victoria showed me the article." Marnie turned to Shane. "She'd have been here but she had a previous function scheduled and couldn't get it switched."

"There was an article in the paper?" Shane asked, confused.

"The article's focus was on all the ways you can volunteer in the community," Sarah-Jane informed him. "I never realized there were so many opportunities."

"It's rewarding to volunteer," Marnie added.

"That was my first time." Shane found himself embarrassed by the admission. "But I'm considering doing it on a regular basis. As well as giving financially to some of the organizations in this community which are on the front lines of helping the disadvantaged."

Lia smiled. "I'm really pleased to hear you say that. You'll be doing so much good."

Shane basked in the warmth of her approval.

"Since when did you decide to become such a big humanitarian?" Sawyer asked, no condemnation in his tone, only curiosity.

"Since I moved to Red Rock." It was the simplest answer. Shane wasn't about to get into the whole adversity-bringing-change-and-character-growth thing he'd discussed with Pastor Tom.

Frankly, he wasn't sure he believed it himself. All he knew was everything that had happened with his father and with Lia was causing him to take a step back and look at life differently.

"Did I tell you that Lia and I are going to a fundraiser for The Red Rock Kitchen at the La Casa Paloma Hotel this Saturday night?" Shane interjected when there was a lull in the conversation.

Marnie's eyes lit up. "Is that the one where they have different kinds of soups in hand-turned pottery bowls made for the event? And, at the end of the evening, you get to keep the bowl?"

"That's the one," Lia said. "It raises a lot of money for good causes."

Marnie glanced at Asher. "We should think about going. I like supporting the community."

Asher glanced at Jace. "We promised Jace we'd take him camping next weekend, remember?"

"That's right. It's going to be fun." Marnie tousled the four-year-old's hair. "Just wait, Lia. It won't be long until your baby is as big as this boy."

Lia patted her stomach, a Madonna-like smile on her lips. "I still can't believe there's a baby in here."

Sarah-Jane took a sip of wine. "When are you due?"

"September 23."

"Do you know what you're having?" Marnie asked.

"Not for sure." Lia stroked the fabric covering her belly. "The doctor thought maybe a girl but she said the baby didn't give them the best view."

"Sounds like a girl to me. Or a stubborn boy." Marnie laughed then turned to Jace. "Are you excited about having a new little cousin?"

Silence descended over the table.

Jace cocked his head and looked at his daddy.

Beside him, Shane could feel the tension rolling off Lia's body in waves.

"I don't think Jace has been around many babies." Asher placed a hand on his son's shoulder. "Have you, pardner?"

The confused expression on the little boy's face eased. "My friend Austin has a new baby brother." Jace's nose wrinkled. "All he does is cry."

"Babies tend to do a lot of that," Lia said lightly, then changed the subject. "This corn bread is delicious. My grandmother used to make hers in a skillet. This tastes so much like hers that it's scary."

The conversation among the women veered off in a culinary direction. Shane relaxed back in his chair and concentrated on eating his dinner.

The special tonight had been quail with sautéed kale and grilled lemons. Lia had opted for a strawberry, avocado and tofu salad, which looked surprisingly tasty. Before they'd entered the dining room, she'd told him she was going to pay her share, but he planned to make sure that didn't happen.

Shane knew Lia didn't have extra cash for dining out. Heck, a couple months ago she didn't have money for eating at all. The thought of her going hungry brought an unfamiliar tightness to his chest.

In the past couple weeks she'd become important to him in a way he couldn't possibly have foreseen.

"Wyatt tells me Jeanne Marie will be here soon," Sarah-Jane said.

Lia looked around the table, her fork poised with a ripe strawberry halfway to her lips. "Who's that?"

"She's a friend of our parents," Shane said before any of his siblings could speak. "She's coming to Red Rock for a visit in a couple weeks."

"I didn't think your parents were here," Lia said, a confused look on her face.

"They aren't," Wyatt explained. "But we're hoping they're back by the time she visits. If not, it'll be a good chance to get better acquainted."

"Do your parents live in Red Rock?" Sarah-Jane asked Lia, apparently realizing her gaffe and eager to change the subject.

"My parents aren't together. I'm not sure where my father is living now. My mother is in Boston." A shadow crossed her face. "We're very close. I miss her a lot."

"Have you ever thought about moving closer to her?" Marnie asked.

Shane took a sip of the pinot noir he'd ordered. What would happen if Lia moved across the country? Having her that far away might be a good thing, he told himself. If it wasn't his baby, then where she lived shouldn't matter at all. If the baby *was* his, once he obtained full custody, it might be better for him—and her—if she lived far away.

His heart quickly rejected both scenarios as unacceptable. Shane realized, despite his best intentions, he'd fallen. And fallen hard.

"Red Rock is my home," Lia answered. "It would take a lot for me to leave."

He glanced over at her and she smiled back at him, a smile that made her brown eyes shimmer.

"Oh, look at that darling baby," Sarah-Jane said as a couple walked by.

She'd spoken so loudly the couple paused.

The father was holding some kind of infant carrier by its handle while his wife—or the woman Shane assumed was his wife—held the baby against her chest. It was impossibly tiny, so small he swore it would fit into a shoe box.

If the pink stretchy bow thing around her softball-size head was any indication, it was a little girl.

"What's her name?" Marnie asked.

"Reece," the woman said proudly. "She's two weeks old today."

"She's so little." Sarah-Jane slanted a glance in Lia's direction. "That's what you'll have soon."

The woman smiled at Lia. "When are you due?"

Lia couldn't seem to take her eyes off the baby. "September 23."

"Reece is so much work," the woman confided. "But we adore her. We can't imagine our life without her in it. I'm sure you and your husband will feel the same way."

"Be prepared not to sleep," the man warned Shane, whose arm rested lightly on the back of Lia's chair.

"We didn't want to hire a nanny," the woman said, almost apologetically. "We wanted to do all the night feedings ourselves."

Night feedings. Nannies. Shane's head spun. He hadn't really thought about Asher's warning that having sole custody of an infant would change his life. Of course, he had the money to hire round-the-clock care. But was that fair to a baby?

After dinner, everyone headed to the parking lot except him and Lia. Since it had finally cooled down outside, she'd told him she wanted to get some walking in so they decided to take a stroll down by the golf course.

The flat shoes she wore tonight were sensible and reminded him of the ballet shoes his sister had worn when they'd all been forced to go as a family to her recitals. His dad had grumbled but he'd always made it a point to be there when his only daughter danced.

Stars dotted the clear night sky. A large moon lit their way. Lia was unusually quiet as they walked, her small hand resting in his.

"It's been a while since I've been around babies," she said softly. "You forget how tiny they are."

"And helpless," Shane added. He couldn't imagine even holding anything that small.

"I want to be a good mother." The brown eyes that met his were serious. "I've been doing a lot of reading on baby care. But I worry if it's going to be enough. Am I going to know what to do? Will I be able to find good child care while I'm at work?"

Lines of worry furrowed her brow and her voice shook slightly.

Shane knew the attorney would say that he should stoke those fears and make her doubt her ability to parent. The problem was, it was *his* ability he was coming to doubt, not hers.

He gave her hand a squeeze. "You'll be an excellent mother."

And he didn't need any P.I. to tell him so.

The lines of worry on her face eased. "Do you really think so?"

He nodded. "You're a warm, loving woman with a good heart."

A ghost of a smile lingered on her lips. "I love her—or him—already."

"I know you do."

"I do think child care might be a problem, though."

Although Shane had no experience with it, he'd over-heard two of the household staff talking about their dif-ficulties in finding someone to watch their kids when the children were sick. "You wouldn't want just anyone watch-ing her."

"That's why my mother keeps encouraging me to move to Boston," Lia said with a sigh. "She said if I was there, she could watch the baby while I worked."

"What did you tell her?"

"I told her that a baby needs a father, too." Lia looked up at him. "And I would never take her away from you."

## Chapter Eleven

By the time she and Shane reached her apartment, waves of exhaustion washed over Lia. She hadn't slept well the night before and her workday had been unusually hectic.

When Shane had asked her to join him for dinner with his family, she'd taken it as a sign that perhaps he was finally ready to accept that he was the father of her baby.

Even though all she'd wanted to do was to go home and put up her feet, she'd told him yes. She had wanted to get better acquainted with his brothers. And she'd never met Sarah-Jane or Marnie.

Lia found it particularly strange that her and Sarah-Jane's paths had never crossed before, considering they shared a love of crafts.

She'd liked them both and had appreciated the way they'd accepted her with open arms. His brothers still looked at her skeptically but at least they were civil.

There had been just one bad moment. When she'd seen

the woman with the baby and realized that she was going to have to do this all on her own. Shane had given no indication that he wanted to be intimately involved with his child's day-to-day life, so all the care would fall on her.

She would handle it. Women did every day. It was just that she railed against the thought of her child being raised by a babysitter. She wanted to be there for her little girl. Or boy.

When they arrived at her apartment, Lia slipped the key from her pocket and opened the door. Then she reached into her purse and pulled out her wallet. "How much do I owe you for dinner tonight?"

"You paid me already."

Lia thought hard, which was especially taxing on such a tired brain. "No. I asked you how much after we finished walking, but you said we could talk about it in the car. I know for sure I never paid you."

"You did," he said with a slight smile. "You gave me the pleasure of your company all evening."

Although the words touched her heart, Lia forced a laugh. "How many women have you used that line on before?"

"None."

"Come on, be honest."

"Seriously, none. Not one woman—before you—has ever concerned herself with paying for dinner."

"I can see that if you're out on a date," Lia said slowly. "But what if you and the woman are just friends?"

"I don't have any women friends," Shane said.

"Yes, you do."

Shane thought for a moment then shook his head. "No. I don't."

She smiled. "You have me."

A softness stole over his masculine features. His blue eyes darkened and he took a step closer.

Her heart picked up speed. He was going to kiss her. And by the look in his eyes and the way she felt whenever he was near, she doubted it would end there.

When he lowered his lips to hers, she turned her face and his lips brushed her cheek.

"You don't want to kiss me?" he murmured against her hair, pulling her close.

"I do," she whispered back.

"Then why turn away?" he asked, his fingers toying with a lock of her hair.

The question had barely left his lips when the door to the apartment across the hall opened and old Mrs. Martinez stuck her head out. "I'd appreciate it if you'd keep it down out there. Some of us have to get up for work in the morning."

"Sorry, Mrs. Martinez," Lia said, sounding properly contrite.

But when Lia turned back to Shane once her neighbor's door shut, her eyes were twinkling. "She had to have her ear pressed against the door to have heard us."

"She's probably got it pressed there now," Shane said in a barely audible tone.

Lia couldn't help but smile. It had been a long day, but a nice one. "Would you like to come in for a few minutes?"

She'd extended the invitation merely to be polite, but he followed her through the open door.

"If you want anything to drink, I'm afraid you're going to have to get it yourself." Lia sank into the well-worn cushions of the sofa and kicked off her shoes.

Shane slipped into the chair opposite her, two lines of worry between his brows. "Are you okay? Can I get you anything?"

She shook her head and smiled wearily. "I'm fine. Just tired."

"Did you mean what you said?" he asked unexpectedly.

Lia had talked so much the entire evening she'd forgotten half of what she'd said. "Remind me."

"About me being your friend."

Lia nodded.

"Good," he said. "Because I like having you as a friend."

"I like having you as a friend, too." A melancholy wistfulness wrapped around Lia's heart. "If I could go back and change one thing, that's what I'd pick."

He looked at her quizzically.

Lia hadn't planned to get into something so heavy this late but it had been on her mind a lot lately. "When a friendship begins, two people do things together, get to know each other's likes and dislikes and share how they feel about important issues. A bond develops and a friendship is born. True?"

"True."

"A relationship begins in much the same way." Lia had given this subject much thought since New Year's Eve, so, despite her tired brain, the words flowed easily. "Except, in a relationship, there's an element of sexual attraction. The way I see it, ideally a couple should be friends before anything of a physical nature occurs. That didn't happen with you and me. The attraction was there, the opportunity was there and we went for it."

"You regret having sex with me." It was a statement more than a question.

Lia glanced down at her slightly rounded belly, determined to be completely honest. "When you saw me in the ranch office and asked me out to dinner, I wished with all my heart it could have simply been two people who were attracted to each other going out and getting to know each other better."

"But you were pregnant."

"I was pregnant. The chance of us having a normal relationship…" She took a deep breath and let it out slowly. "Well, that train has left the station."

"I believe we can pull that train back into the station anytime we want."

Lia looked at him. "I don't understand."

"I'm suggesting we start over," he said. "This time we do it right."

Lia twisted her lips in a wry smile. "Going back is impossible."

He shook his head. "Think about it. Isn't that what we've been doing the past couple of weeks?"

She met his gaze. "You really think it's an option?"

He gave a decisive nod and she found his confidence contagious.

The thought of a do-over held infinite appeal. Of course, they couldn't completely start over—some things couldn't be undone—but the thought of getting to know Shane better, of having him really and truly consider her a friend instead of an enemy…well, the thought brought tears to her eyes.

She stuck out her hand. "Hi, I'm Natalia Serrano."

What he and Lia discussed was never far from Shane's thoughts the next day. Would he have pursued a relationship, even a friendship, with her back in January? Perhaps, but it would have been difficult. After all, he'd left town the next day to take care of business in Atlanta and to search for Jeanne Marie.

Now that he was back in Red Rock, was he interested? The attorney would say Shane should be definitely interested. He needed to get to know Lia in order to build a case against her if the child she was carrying turned out to be his.

But that wasn't what this thing with Lia was about, at least not any longer. He liked Lia. Liked the way she could be strong willed, yet willing to bend. Liked her optimistic attitude and the pure joy she seemed to get from life.

If last night had been their first encounter, she'd definitely be a woman he'd want to know better. He glanced at his cell phone lying on the desk.

It was much too soon to call if a relationship was what he wanted. But they'd talked about building a friendship. And there was no game-playing in friendship. He picked up the phone and punched in her number.

When she answered, he had to smile at her businesslike tone.

"Natalia," he said, because this was a new friendship and that was the name she'd given him. "This is Shane Fortune. We met last night."

A moment of stunned surprise, then a little laugh.

"Shane, yes, I remember." She lowered her voice. "How nice to hear from you."

"I realize it's short notice, but a business acquaintance told me about a great German restaurant in Fredericksburg. I wondered if you might be interested in having dinner there tonight with me." The moment the words left his mouth, Shane wondered if he should have been less specific. Perhaps Lia didn't like German food.

"Well," she said slowly, "I've been craving sauerbraten. And I do need some peaches."

Shane held the phone out from his ear and wondered if there was a problem with the connection. "Peaches?"

"Fredericksburg and the surrounding area produce about half of the peach crop in the state," Lia informed him.

"Is that a yes?" he asked, his heart quickening like a schoolboy's.

"Absolutely." The happiness in her voice made him smile.

"Great. I'll pick you up at your place at two."

"Two?" He could almost hear the frown in her voice. "I don't get off until five."

"Since we just met, I'm not sure if you're aware of the fact that your boss is my brother." Shane leaned back in the desk chair, enjoying the conversation. "He's giving you the entire afternoon off, with pay."

He heard a sound and looked up to find Sawyer standing in the doorway to his office. Shane motioned him inside.

"In fact, he's with me now. Do you need to talk with him? Hear it from him directly?"

"No. No. I believe you," Lia said hurriedly. "So I'm through for the day at noon?"

"That's right," Shane said. "And dress casual."

"Okay," she said, sounding breathless. "And, Shane?"

"Yes."

"I'm glad you called. I was hoping to hear from you again."

When he clicked off, Shane couldn't keep from smiling.

"What was that about?" Sawyer took a seat in one of the chairs in front of the desk.

"Lia and I have decided to be friends." Satisfaction surged through Shane's body. "By the way, you've given her the afternoon off. She and I are going to pick peaches in Fredericksburg and have sauerbraten."

"Who are you?" Sawyer leaned forward. "And what have you done with my brother?"

Shane found the sight of his normally implacable brother completely flummoxed, amusing.

"Last night Lia and I decided we'd jumped into...

things…before we'd had a chance to get to know each other." Shane wondered if he should take the car to Fredericksburg or perhaps the pickup would be better if they would be bringing back peaches. "We've decided to spend time together and get better acquainted."

The hour or so drive north would be pleasurable. There were so many facets to Lia and he'd barely touched the surface.

"Smart move," Sawyer said with an approving smile. "For a second I thought you'd lost your edge, but once again you proved me wrong."

Shane cocked his head.

"You knew she'd be on her guard," Sawyer continued, "thereby limiting the amount of information you'd be able to get from her. But in a new friendship, the emphasis is on getting to know each other. A brilliant strategy, but then I wouldn't expect anything less from you."

Shane quickly considered his options. He could tell his brother that he'd gotten this all wrong. But then Sawyer might decide Shane had lost his good sense and refuse to let Lia off work. As dedicated as she was to her job, he knew she'd never take the time off if Sawyer didn't approve.

Shane pushed back his chair and simply smiled.

## Chapter Twelve

The German restaurant on Main Street in Fredericksburg had both indoor and outdoor seating. Though Lia was hot from their excursions to several peach orchards, when the hostess asked if they wanted to sit outside, she blurted out yes before Shane could even ask her preference.

"We'll sit outside," he told the hostess, who'd been eyeing him with an appreciative gleam in her eye.

Lia could completely understand. Although beads of perspiration had run down her cheeks while they'd filled buckets with peaches, Shane had looked as if he'd been sitting inside an office all day.

His khaki shorts were still crisp and his blue polo shirt looked as if he'd just taken it off a hanger. Lia was happy she'd paired a black top with tiny white stars to go with her yellow shorts. At least the black didn't show the dirt… as much.

"Are you and your…wife enjoying your time in Fredericksburg?" the tall blonde hostess asked.

*Really,* Lia wanted to say to her, *you're hitting on a guy who's out with a pregnant woman?*

She caught the woman glancing first at her left hand, then at Shane's, but Lia had never thought she'd be so bold.

Shane rested one hand lightly on Lia's back and pulled out her chair with his other. "We're having a wonderful time."

The blonde's face fell. "Good to hear."

Once they were seated, Shane lifted the menu.

"Does that happen to you often?" Lia asked.

"What?"

"Women throwing themselves at you?"

He gave a humorless chuckle. "Let's just say it's not an infrequent occurrence."

"How do you feel about it?" Lia leaned forward, resting her elbows on the table. "Do you find it annoying or flattering?"

The waitress arrived then and it wasn't until after she'd taken their order and brought their drinks—water for Lia and a stout German beer for Shane—that he answered her question.

"When you grow up in a family like mine, people often like you for your money. Or for what they think you can do for them."

Though his tone gave nothing away, a tiny muscle in his jaw jumped.

"Isn't it easy to spot them?" she asked.

He took a sip from the mug. "Not always."

"How do you find out the truth?"

"Things become clear."

"C'mon, that tells me absolutely nothing. When was the first time you knew a woman was with you more for the money than for you?"

"Ah, that would have been my first girlfriend." Shane's

lips twisted in a semblance of a smile. "Amber was fifteen. I was sixteen. We were classmates at Choate. She was there on scholarship."

"Choate?"

"A private school in Connecticut."

"What happened?"

"I fell head over heels for her. She told me she loved me. We became intimate," he explained in a voice devoid of emotion. "Then her mom went to my father and threatened to charge me with statutory rape."

Lia gasped. "But it had been consensual."

"Didn't matter." The flash of pain in his eyes was so brief, Lia wondered if she'd only imagined it. "Our attorney discovered that in Connecticut, having sex with anyone under sixteen is illegal. My father paid her off—which is what her mother wanted all along—so I wouldn't be charged."

"Could they have even proved you'd had sex?"

"She was a day student and lived in Hamden. We did it one time in her bedroom while her mom was at work," Shane continued in a matter-of-fact tone. "Her mother had hidden a camera in the room. She got it all on tape."

"Unbelievable."

"It was my introduction to the real world," he said with a cynical laugh.

"That's a crazy example," Lia said. "And really more of the mother being out for what she could get, than the girl."

Shane shrugged. "Amber seemed to like the new clothes and convertible they bought with the money. I doubt she missed me at all."

A heavy pall settled over the table.

"I've never had that problem." Lia gave a laugh. "But I have had a few guys come on a little strong. They seemed to think the poor little Latina would give them anything they wanted just because they had a nice car or were on the football team."

"Jerks." The muscle in Shane's jaw jumped again.

Lia took a sip of ice water. "I knew how to say no and make them believe it. If they persisted, I had an older brother who didn't like anyone messing with his baby sister."

"You grew up poor?" he asked after a long moment.

She nodded. "The strange thing is, until I reached high school, I didn't realize it."

He lifted a questioning brow.

"I had my own bedroom. How can you be poor if you have your own bedroom?" Lia saw no need to mention her brothers slept on a pullout sofa bed in the living room. "Our neighbors were hardworking people living the American dream. Like us, they owned their own home. There were barbecues in the summer and Christmas caroling in the winter. When I'd hear things on the news about the disadvantaged, I never thought it applied to me. Then I went to high school."

"What happened?"

"Lots of rich kids."

"You envied them."

"What? No." Her lips twisted. "Well, maybe just a little. I envied the clothes and cars and the fact that they didn't have to clean houses after they got home from school. But I had a loving family and lots of friends."

"And your own bedroom."

Lia smiled. "I was rich in all the ways that matter."

"How was college?"

"It was harder because I was away from my family for the first time." Lia's lips lifted in a wistful smile. "But my college roommate became my best friend. That made all the difference. She was also there on a scholarship, so she understood how to scrimp. But she hated doing without. If anyone was driven to obtain the finer things in life, it was her."

"Where is she now?"

"In San Antonio." Lia thought of the road Stephanie had taken and sorrow filled her. "We still see each other twice a year for our birthdays. She was the one who called the other night. Her birthday is this month and we're trying to find a date and time to get together to celebrate."

"My brothers have always been my closest friends," Shane said. "You know you can trust family."

The waitress brought their food and for the next fifteen minutes or so the conversation became more casual. The sauerbraten was so good Lia had to force herself to eat slowly. Shane appeared to enjoy his Wiener schnitzel.

She learned that Shane had been sent to board at Choate when he was fourteen. He discovered that she'd played the flute and still had it in her apartment. But the last time she'd brought it out and tried to play it, her neighbor had called the police.

They laughed and talked, and didn't leave the table until the sun had begun to set. He took her hand on the way to the truck. She laced her fingers through his because it felt so right.

But as pleasurable as the evening had been, by the time he pulled to a stop in front of her apartment, Lia was having difficulty keeping her eyes open.

"I think I kept my new friend out too late," he said with a smile.

"I hardly think ten o'clock qualifies as late." She covered a yawn with her hand. "But I'm ready for bed."

"I could pretend that I'm one of the guys from high school and take that as an invitation to join you," Shane said with a teasing smile.

"And then I'd have to slam the door in your face," Lia shot back, "and call my brother."

He laughed out loud then gave her a warning glance as she reached for the door handle.

"Wait." Shane shut off the truck and pocketed the keys. "I'll open that for you."

"You don't have to—" Lia began but stopped. The look on his face told her protesting was pointless.

After he helped her out of the truck, he walked to the back of the vehicle and pulled out two buckets filled with peaches.

"I don't need two," she protested. "One is plenty."

But he just smiled and when they reached her floor, he stopped at the door across the hall.

Mrs. Martinez, the older woman who'd so soundly chastised them for talking too loudly the other night, cracked her door open in response to his knock. "Yes?"

"We brought you some fresh peaches, ma'am." Shane held out the buckets. "Natalia and I thought you might enjoy them."

The woman's eyes widened at the sight of the plump, sweet-smelling fruit. She smiled, actually *smiled,* at Lia. "Well, thank you very much. I certainly do enjoy fresh peaches."

"They're from Fredericksburg," Lia told her.

"Then I know they'll be good." The woman shifted her gaze to Shane. "You both have a nice evening. Thank you, again."

When she shut the door, Shane and Lia exchanged a smile.

"I'm embarrassed I didn't think to reach out to her before." Lia glanced curiously at him. "Yet you did, even after how she acted the other night."

He shot her a wink. "Being around you seems to bring out the best in me."

A warmth wrapped itself around Lia's heart. "I can't remember receiving a nicer compliment."

"Then you're hanging out with the wrong people."

She unlocked her apartment and pushed the door open before turning back to Shane. "Want to come in for a few minutes?"

"I'll put the bucket in the kitchen," he said, stepping inside. "It's too heavy for you to carry."

After he'd deposited the peaches, he was almost to the door when she grabbed his hand. "What's the hurry?"

He smiled. "You need your sleep."

"Don't I get a good-night kiss?"

Desire flared in his eyes but he hesitated.

"There's nothing wrong with a little kiss between friends," Lia said in a throaty whisper that, even to her ears, sounded surprisingly sensual.

Shane slipped his arms around her shoulders and pulled her close. "Since you put it that way…"

His mouth closed over hers in a gentle, sweet kiss that ended all too soon. "Sleep tight, Lia."

She followed him to the door. "Shane?"

He turned back toward her. "Yes?"

"I had a nice time tonight."

"So did I." He smiled. "Sleep tight."

From the doorway, Lia watched him until he disappeared from view. Then she returned to her apartment, making sure to lock the door behind her.

She'd meant what she said to Shane. Today had marked a shift in their relationship. From the moment she'd first seen him in that deserted courtyard, she'd been attracted to him.

Not only was he good-looking, there had been something about his quiet confidence that drew her to him. When she was with him, she felt safe and protected.

But physical attraction on its own, no matter how compelling, wasn't enough for a relationship. She had to like the person, had to enjoy their company and had to know what made them tick.

Tonight she'd found that with Shane. Granted, they'd barely scratched the surface. But it was a good start and she found herself humming as she headed to the shower, wondering just where this friendship would take them.

Shane brought the rest of the peaches into the house and left a note for the cook before heading for the stairs. Once he reached his room, he realized it was too early for bed. Besides, there were too many emotions and thoughts tugging at him. Even if he was tired, he knew sleep would not come easily. So he pulled on his running shoes and headed outside.

Running in the dark held its share of risks but there was a full moon out tonight and the driveway up to the ranch house was familiar terrain.

He'd just stepped off the porch when he heard Sawyer call his name.

He muttered a curse under his breath. The last person he was in the mood to speak with tonight was his brother. But he obligingly turned around and headed to where Sawyer waited on the porch. "Need something?"

"You're spending a lot of time lately with Ms. Serrano." Sawyer's tone made it clear he didn't approve.

"I'm getting to know her better." Shane smiled. "Wasn't that the plan?"

"You need to be careful."

"If you've got something to say, bro, just say it."

"She's an attractive woman. All that dark hair. Those

big brown puppy-dog eyes." Sawyer's eyes met his. "It would be easy for a man to fall for her."

"Is that what this is about?" Shane scoffed. "You think I can't handle myself? You think I don't know the score?"

"I think we can know the score and still be tempted to believe in a person, to think they're different than they are…"

"Don't worry about me, little brother. My eyes are wide open."

Shane figured he must have been convincing because Sawyer went back inside.

*Eyes wide open,* he'd told Sawyer.

He swore and started running.

Over the next two weeks, Shane saw Lia every day. The soup fundraiser that Saturday was only the beginning. They had lunch together by the pool, explored several other small towns in the area and danced in a variety of honky-tonks to some good and not-so-good music. One night he took her to hear the San Antonio Symphony. The performance was in the historic Majestic Theatre, a 1920s theater that had been carefully restored to its original splendor.

Shane had suggested they get dessert afterward at one of the restaurants in the area. But when Lia told him she was craving strawberry ice cream, they ended up having cones instead.

They spent one Sunday just strolling through the Botanical Gardens. Last night, he and Lia had gone to the San Antonio Rodeo and it had been almost midnight by the time he'd dropped her off.

He whistled as he bounded down the stairs for breakfast. Sawyer was already at the table, a plate of food before him. He looked up when Shane entered the room.

"What's for breakfast?" Shane asked his brother.

"Peaches." Sawyer groaned. "How many buckets of those blasted things did you bring back from Fredericksburg?"

"Shh," Shane said as Carmen, the cook, brought his plate and set it before him.

"This looks very good," Shane said politely. "What is it?"

"It's a peach-and-sausage breakfast square, sir." The older woman beamed. "I made the crust out of a pancake mix. It's my own recipe."

"It looks delicious," Shane said, giving her an approving smile.

"Suck-up," Sawyer muttered under his breath, low enough for only Shane to hear. He forked off a piece and took a bite. He chewed thoughtfully for a second or two. "It is good. Though after all the peaches are gone, I don't think I'll want to see anything with fruit for a long, long time."

"I have a conference call at ten," Shane said. "I'm going to invite Lia to the house for lunch. She'll need the break."

"I've noticed you're very—" Sawyer paused as if searching for the right word "—*solicitous* of her."

Shane added a dash of cream to his coffee. "She *is* pregnant."

"Odds are it's not your baby."

Shane tightened his fingers around the coffee cup. "We were out late last night and yet she was here bright and early this morning."

"She's not your responsibility."

"She may not be my responsibility, but I care for her as a person," Shane said through gritted teeth. "Is that a crime?"

"It is if you aren't careful. We've both seen how women can pretend to be something they're not to try to land themselves a Fortune. The obvious gold diggers are easy to spot. The pros look very much like the real deal."

Shane took a sip of coffee. He hated his brother for bringing his doubts back to the forefront. But most of all he hated himself for believing that Lia was exactly who she appeared to be.

## Chapter Thirteen

The PB and J that Lia had brought with her to the office went back in the brown bag when Shane invited her to join him at the ranch house for lunch. Instead of the kitchen, they'd taken their meal in the dining room with Carmen, the Fortunes' cook, serving them.

"This side dish was fabulous," Lia told the woman as she picked up their plates. "A perfect accompaniment to the grilled chicken."

"Thank you." The rotund woman, her black hair streaked with gray and pulled back in a single braid, beamed. "It's a new recipe. It's called Grilled Peaches Jezebel."

The sweet yet tangy taste lingered on Lia's tongue. Though she liked to cook, she didn't often take the time. And it was never as much fun cooking for one. "I'm having difficulty pinpointing the ingredients. Honey? Maybe a little mustard?"

Carmen nodded approvingly. "The marinade is a mixture of honey, mustard and horseradish."

"Horseradish." Lia shook her head. She'd never have guessed that one. "Odd, but it works."

"You should make it for Sawyer," Shane told Carmen, an odd glint in his eyes. "He loves anything with peaches."

Carmen's lips twitched even as she nodded and cleared away the last of the dishes. "I'll get the dessert."

Though her stomach signaled full, Lia decided she might be able to manage a bite or two of something sweet. She took a sip of iced tea, leaned back in the chair and let herself relax. The shades at the window were partially drawn, protecting the room against the heat of midday.

Her eyelids wanted to flutter closed. By the time she'd gotten ready for bed last night and picked up the apartment, it had been nearly one. The alarm went off at five.

She knew she should be getting more sleep but she was having too much fun. The past couple of weeks had been a roller-coaster ride of emotions. She'd loved spending time with Shane. He was smart and funny and considerate, not to mention sexy as all get-out.

Of course, because they'd decided the focus was on friendship, they'd limited their physical intimacy to a good-night kiss. But those kisses had been getting longer. Last night's kiss had lasted almost an hour. She'd been oh-so-tempted to ask him to stay the night.

She'd resisted, but barely. And now, conscious of those blue-on-blue eyes focused on her, she found herself tempted by him again.

"You have shadows under your eyes." Shane leaned close and brushed the area lightly with the pads of his thumbs, the skin sizzling beneath his touch. "You're dead on your feet."

"Thanks for the compliment," Lia said with a wry smile.

"I'm worried about you," he said softly. "And about the baby."

For a second she thought he might be implying that she wasn't taking good care of herself, but when she looked at his face, all she saw was concern. For her. For their unborn child. Her heart lurched.

She glanced at her wrist and stretched. "I still have fifteen minutes to recharge."

Pushing back his chair, Shane stood and held out a hand. "Then we'll take our dessert in the living room where you can sit on the sofa and put your feet up."

His wicked grin made her wonder if rest and relaxation were all he had in mind.

Ten minutes later she sat in the living room with a half-eaten bowl of peach cobbler on her lap and the taste of Shane on her lips. She offered him another spoonful of cobbler. Once he took a bite, he'd get a kiss. Then it would be his turn to feed the cobbler to her…and get a kiss. Lia had to admit she liked the game almost as much as the sweet peaches and whipped cream.

But before Shane's mouth could close around the spoon, Sawyer strode into the room. Lia knew her boss's sharp and assessing gaze missed nothing. Not Shane's thigh pressed tightly against hers, not his arm looped intimately around her shoulders, nor the slight trace of red gloss from a kiss that had missed its mark. Sawyer's lips tightened.

Though she and Shane had been doing nothing wrong, heat rose to Lia's cheeks. She pushed to her feet, dropping the spoon into the bowl and placing it on the end table. "I was just getting ready to head back to the office."

Sawyer nodded curtly then focused on his brother. "There's a phone call I believe you'll want to take. It's Jeanne Marie. She says it's important."

Shane rose and his brows pulled together. "Why did she call you if she wanted to speak with me?"

"She didn't." Sawyer held out the phone. "You left your phone in the other room. I heard it ring and noticed her name on the screen so I answered. She wouldn't tell me why she's calling."

In two steps, Shane was at his brother's side, lifting the phone from his hand.

"I have it on Mute," Sawyer told him.

Shane took one last glance at Lia. "Are you okay?"

Lia scrambled awkwardly to her feet, smoothing the wrinkles from her skirt. "I need to get back to work."

"I'll call you later," Shane said, then immediately refocused on the phone. "Jeanne Marie, it's good to hear from you."

The rest of his words faded as he strode down the hall.

"Jeanne Marie." Lia tried to comb through her tangled hair with her fingers. "She's a family friend, right?"

A muscle in Sawyer's jaw twitched. "Is that what Shane told you?"

She nodded, surprised at the suspicion in his eyes. What was his problem?

"You ask a lot of questions," Sawyer said flatly. "About things that are none of your business."

Lia felt as if she'd been slapped. She blinked back unexpected tears before he could notice.

"I just don't want to see my brother hurt," he said as she grabbed her shoes and brushed past him.

"Shane is more than capable of looking out for himself," she said over her shoulder, not turning back.

"I'm not so sure," she heard Sawyer murmur as she exited the room. "Not anymore."

All week Lia had been looking forward to attending the annual Red Rock Spring Fling. When Shane pulled the truck into the dirt parking lot on the outskirts of town, she expected them to talk about what rides they'd go on or debate whether a funnel cake topped with apples could be considered a fruit.

Instead Shane brought up the subject of her moving to New Fortunes Ranch...again.

"I'm not moving in with you," Lia said as she took his hand and stepped out of the pickup. "So quit asking."

"I don't like where you're living," he said in an equally firm tone. "It's not safe."

Though the crime rate in Red Rock was low, Lia couldn't deny that most of the recent assaults had occurred within a mile of her apartment. Still, she felt safe in her neighborhood. Or relatively safe.

The mulish expression on her face must have told Shane he wasn't making any headway, so he changed tactics. "Think how much easier life would be with us being under the same roof. Instead of my driving into town to drop you off, we could just walk up the stairs."

"It would be even more convenient if we were in the same bedroom. That way, if you thought of something you wanted to say to me, you wouldn't need to call," Lia said with a heavy dose of sarcasm. She wondered when he was going to concede defeat on this topic. Knowing his tenacity, probably never.

"Now we're on the same page." Shane slipped an arm around her shoulders, a movement that had come to feel so natural.

"I love carnivals," Lia said, changing the subject as they approached the entrance to the festival.

"Judging by the crowd, this is definitely the place to be." Shane pulled her close, shielding her with his body as a drunk cowboy stumbled past.

His whole family would be at the carnival tonight. They

knew he was now seeing Lia regularly. While his brothers were still suspicious of her motives—especially Sawyer—Shane's own concerns about her lying to him had vanished. Which was funny considering he was the one with the most to lose.

Yet, he wasn't worried. From spending time with her, he was convinced deliberate deceit wasn't in her.

He believed the more his family knew her, the more they'd accept and like her. That was why he was eager to throw them together as much as possible. Even if they didn't run across his siblings at the carnival, they planned to gather at Wyatt's house later in the evening.

"I love the rides." Lia gazed at the multicolored lights with a wistful expression. "But I don't think the jerky motion would be good for the baby."

"What about the Ferris wheel?" Shane suggested. "That's pretty tame."

"You don't want to go on the Ferris wheel," Lia said, even as her gaze lingered on the brightly lit wheel. "You're just being nice."

Normally the thought of getting on a ride with all the excitement of a rocking chair wouldn't have appealed to Shane. But the longing in her eyes made him change his mind.

"Actually, I would." He fingered a strand of her long dark hair. "It'd be fun to kiss you at the top, under the stars."

"You're not into public displays of affection," Lia reminded him.

"Not true. I've got my arm around your shoulder," Shane said lightly. "We hold hands all the time in public."

"You're right." Two bright patches of pink colored her cheeks. "Forget I said anything."

"I'm not ashamed to be seen with you."

She looked up in startled surprise. That was when he knew he'd correctly read her thoughts.

"I understand, you know," she said quickly, the pink in her cheeks deepening to a dusky rose. "Your family is a big deal in this town. I'm a Latina born on the wrong side of the tracks. And I'm pregnant, to boot."

"There is so much wrong with what you're saying—" Shane pressed his lips together and counted to five "—that I'm not sure where to start."

"Hey, want to go on the roller coaster with us?"

Shane turned to find his brother Wyatt standing by a snow-cone booth, Sarah-Jane at his side, her long auburn hair pulled back in a complicated braid.

"I love your cowboy hat," Lia said, eyeing the black Stetson on the tall man who looked as if he was Texas-born.

Wyatt smiled at Lia with surprising warmth. He lifted the hat off his head and plopped it down on hers. "It's yours."

She reached up to tug it off, but Sarah-Jane placed a restraining hand on her arm. "Take it. Trust me, he has dozens more at home." Sarah-Jane cast a teasing glance at Wyatt. "And you look better in it anyway."

Wyatt growled in mock outrage and Lia giggled.

"Just for that," Wyatt said to his fiancée, "we're sitting in the very front of the roller coaster."

Sarah-Jane smiled smugly. "My favorite spot."

"That's not why we're sitting there," Wyatt insisted.

"Whatever you say," she said, her eyes filled with laughter.

Shane couldn't believe what he'd just witnessed. He'd never seen his brother act so, well, so goofy.

Wyatt cast a pointed glance at Shane and Lia. "We're planning on you coming over later tonight."

"If I'm not too tired—" Lia began.

"We're toasting marshmallows over an open fire and making s'mores," Sarah-Jane said in a persuasive tone.

Lia brought a finger to her lips and pretended to think. "Ah. In that case, I'll be there."

"That's what I thought." Unexpectedly Sarah-Jane reached over and briefly embraced Lia. "I'm so happy you're coming."

Wyatt opened his arms to Lia, a devilish gleam in his eyes. "I'd like to give you a hug, too."

Shane punched his brother in the arm. "You've got your own girlfriend. Leave mine alone."

Girlfriend. Was that what Lia was now? His girlfriend?

Wyatt grinned and captured Sarah-Jane's hand. "Come on, woman. The roller coaster awaits."

"Your brother seems in a good mood tonight." A smile lingered on Lia's lips as they watched the two disappear into the crowd.

"He's got it bad for Sarah-Jane," Shane observed, wondering if Wyatt would say the same thing about him with Lia. For some reason the thought didn't bother him.

"I can see why," Lia said. "She's a nice person."

"Uncle Shane." A young voice rang out and Shane turned to find his nephew Jace racing toward him at full speed.

When the little boy drew close, Shane snatched Jace up in his arms and swung him around until the child was laughing hard.

"I don't know if I'd do that," Asher warned. "He just ate a whole bag of cotton candy."

Marnie took a step back. "And drank a soda."

Shane stopped midswing.

"Please, Uncle Shane, do it some more," Jace protested when Shane set him back down on the ground.

"That's enough for now." Shane remembered a long-ago day when his father had ignored his mother's warning and kept swinging him. What happened next hadn't been pretty. "What rides have you gone on, buckaroo?"

Distracted, the boy launched into a detailed accounting of each and every ride.

"We're going to give the merry-go-round a try next." Asher took his son's hand and turned toward his brother. "You two headed that way?"

"Opposite direction." Shane glanced at Lia and inhaled the clean, fresh scent of her. Her hair shimmered like rich dark mahogany in the sunlight. Dressed in blue jeans and boots with a bright orange shirt and her hair pulled back, she looked like a sexy cowgirl. *My sexy cowgirl,* he thought with a burst of possessive pride. "We're going on the Ferris wheel."

"I like Ferris wheels." With outstretched arms Jace dipped and swooped like an airplane. "It goes all the way to the clouds, doesn't it, Daddy?"

"That's right, son." Asher shifted his glance to Shane. "I seem to remember you making several derisive comments about that particular ride in the past."

Shane rested his hand on Lia's shoulder. "It's all in who you're with."

"I find them very romantic." Marnie gazed at Asher through lowered lids and spoke in a low tone. "I've always fantasized about being kissed at the top of a Ferris wheel."

"What did Marnie say, Daddy?" Jace's arms dropped to his sides. "She whispered. You told me it's not nice to whisper."

"I'm sorry, Jace," Marnie said, looking surprisingly contrite.

Asher crouched down in front of his son. "Marnie wants me to take her to the top of the Ferris wheel and rock the cab back and forth really fast."

Jace's eyes widened. "That would scare me."

"If we do that, I'll have you stay on the ground with Uncle Shane or Uncle Wyatt."

Shane exchanged a smile with Lia.

"We'd be happy to watch Jace when you, ah, take your Ferris wheel ride," Shane offered. "Just call when you need me."

They talked for a few more minutes before Asher, Marnie and Jace headed to the merry-go-round and Shane and Lia headed toward the double Ferris wheel.

On the way they passed various red-and-white-striped tents filled with games of chance.

"Ooh, look at that gorgeous bear." Lia stopped to stare at the giant stuffed animal with a yellow bow around its neck. Her gaze grew wistful. "I always wanted one of those when I was a kid."

"Hey, buddy, win the little lady a great big bear. Just hit the right balloon and that bear is hers."

Normally Shane would have walked right by, ignoring the sales patter from the carnival barker, but he couldn't ignore the yearning in Lia's eyes.

The game was a balloon dart throw. Though Shane hadn't played before, he knew to be successful he had to have a strategy. He picked up the dart and felt the tip.

Dull.

It appeared finesse was out—a strong throw was in.

He studied the white board with all the balloons fluttering in the light breeze.

"Are you going to throw or look at it all day?" the man blustered. "Perhaps the little lady should try her luck."

The sign proclaimed a prize behind every balloon. But all prizes weren't equal. Since most people aimed for the middle, it stood to reason that the bigger gifts would be on the outer edge. Shane didn't want to win Lia a trinket—he wanted the bear.

Balancing the dart between his fingers, he took aim at a balloon at the very bottom right corner of the board and threw as hard as he could.

The red balloon popped and Lia clapped her hands.

"What did you win?" She leaned forward and he inhaled the tantalizing scent of Chanel.

He grinned. "The bear, of course."

The barker forced a smile and grabbed the large stuffed animal, handing it to Shane.

The man tried to get him to play again but Shane simply shook his head and took Lia's arm. Once they were out of the man's earshot, he presented the prize to Lia. "This is for you. And for the baby."

"Her first gift." Tears filled Lia's eyes.

He stroked her arm. "Hey, I wouldn't have won it for you if I knew it'd make you cry."

She swiped at the tears with the pads of her fingers. "I'm just happy. I can't remember having so much fun at a carnival before."

Shane agreed. He hadn't been all that excited about coming tonight, but he was enjoying himself. "Ready for the Ferris wheel?"

A smile lifted her lips. "The night just keeps getting better and better."

Though his parents had gone out of their way to instill good manners in all their children, whenever Shane was around Lia, his concern went beyond manners. He wanted to ease her burdens, take the weight from her shoulders, be her knight in shining armor. Could this be what love felt like?

"Let me carry this for you." Shane reached for the stuffed animal.

*CINDY KIRK*

157

Lia shook her head and tightened her hold on the bear. "I don't want to let him go. Thank you for winning him, Shane. You're the best."

Last year Shane had closed several difficult multimillion-dollar deals in one day. He'd thought nothing could eclipse the high he'd felt then. But now, having Lia look at him with her heart in her eyes, he realized he'd been wrong.

The line for the Ferris wheel moved quickly. When they stepped into the gondola, Lia started to settle the bear between them, but Shane lifted it to the other side of her. He didn't want anything keeping them apart.

If someone had told him six months ago that he'd be at the Red Rock Spring Fling winning a teddy bear and riding a Ferris wheel, he'd have told them they were crazy.

But being here with Lia, well, it felt good.

"You were right," he murmured, holding her hand securely in his as their gondola began its upward ascent.

"About Ferris wheels?" When Lia looked up at him with those big brown eyes, he almost forgot what he'd been about to say.

"About the importance of becoming friends before becoming lovers." His gaze searched hers. "We needed to get to know each other, to care for each other, before we made love again."

The gondola lurched. She clutched his hand tightly.

He slipped his other arm around her shoulders, pulling her even closer. "Don't worry. I won't ever let anything happen to you."

The vehemence in his voice seemed to surprise her, but Shane meant every word. Over the past weeks, Lia had burrowed her way into his heart, and he would move heaven and earth to protect her.

"Shane," she said as the Ferris wheel took on more passengers and their gondola inched its way toward the sky. "You said we needed to care for each other before we made love again."

"That's right."

"I care for you."

"And I care for you."

He didn't need to say more. When they reached the top and his lips closed over hers, they both knew how the evening was going to end.

## Chapter Fourteen

"Did you and Marnie ever go on the Ferris wheel?" Shane asked Asher later that evening by the fire pit in Wyatt's backyard.

Instead of immediately answering, Asher handed him a bottle of Dos Equis then turned to Lia and held up a tumbler filled with bubbling clear liquid. "Club soda?"

"I'd love some." Lia smiled her thanks.

Only after Asher handed her the drink did he turn back to Shane.

"Actually—" Asher gazed at his son, who stood nearby eating a burned marshmallow "—the three of us went together."

"There were three on our ride, too," Lia said with an impish smile. "Shane won me a huge teddy bear."

Sawyer lifted a brow. "You always said those games are rigged."

Shane ignored his brother's comment. He glanced at

Lia, a smile lifting the corners of his lips. "For an accountant, your math skills appear a bit rusty. There were four on our ride."

Lia held up a hand and counted off on her fingers. "You, me, the bear..."

"The baby," Shane prompted.

"Oh, that's right." Lia was surprised he'd brought up the baby in front of his siblings. Even though she was "blooming" more every day, she'd noticed Shane rarely mentioned her pregnancy when they were with other people.

"We've got s'mores over here," Wyatt called out.

"Lots and lots of s'mores," Sarah-Jane echoed. "Come and get them before the chocolate melts."

"I'm interested." Shane held out his hand to her. "You?"

Were his blue eyes darker, his gaze more intense this evening? And was his question about something other than s'mores?

Lia shivered, sensing change in the air. It felt as if her and Shane's relationship had been chugging along a certain path only to shift into high gear this evening. She took his hand. "I'm definitely interested."

For the rest of the evening, Shane never left her side. Lia munched on s'mores and eagerly ingested stories Shane and his brothers shared of their childhood.

She got a good view of the men they were now from those stories. It appeared Shane had always been the responsible, serious one. The child upon whose shoulders his father had placed the greatest expectations.

There was certainly tension whenever any of the boys mentioned their dad. Lia made a mental note to ask Shane about it later.

One by one, the couples excused themselves to return home. Shane took her hand as they strolled to the car. The night had been perfect and she was reluctant to see it end.

When they reached the truck, instead of opening the door, Shane turned her to face him, pressing her back against the door. "Ever since the Ferris wheel, I've wanted to do this again."

As his lips closed over hers, Lia inhaled the intoxicating scent of him, reveling in the strength of his arms around her. Her fingers sank softly into his dark hair.

But one kiss wasn't enough for either of them. Before long the sweet, gentle pressure morphed into something more carnal, something almost desperate.

"Get a room," she heard someone call out.

Shane stiffened and Lia thought he might step back. Instead he planted little kisses along her jaw and laced his fingers through hers. When she looked up, his eyes were dark and filled with need.

"I want you," he murmured, his lips moving along her cheek to her earlobe. "Stay with me tonight."

She thought of all the reasons she shouldn't, but those reasons didn't matter. Tonight she wanted to love him with her body as she already loved him with her heart. "Yes."

His head jerked back, startled surprise in his eyes. "What did you say?"

She kissed him lightly on the lips. "I said I want to spend the night with you."

On the short drive to his place, Lia's body hummed with excitement. Unlike New Year's Eve, this time she was sure of her decision. There would be no indecision or second-guessing.

The only bad moment came when they were climbing the stairs to Shane's suite of rooms and ran into Sawyer. Lia saw the disapproval in his eyes. Shane didn't appear to notice. He greeted his brother and kept walking.

"Sawyer doesn't approve," Lia whispered as Shane

opened a door at the end of a long hall and stepped back to let her enter.

"Forget him." He pulled his bedroom door shut and twisted the lock. "All that matters is you and me."

Shane gently released her hair from its clip so it hung loose around her shoulders. He took a step back, holding her at arm's length. "You are so beautiful."

Lia gave a little laugh. "What I am is hot and dusty."

"If you're inviting me to shower with you—" Shane's eyes glittered "—I say yes."

She let him take her hand and tug her into a large bathroom that rivaled the one in the hotel.

There were mirrors everywhere. Though washing off all the grime from the day sounded heavenly, she doubted Shane planned to turn off the light, which meant he would get a good view of her rapidly changing body.

By the time she'd unbuttoned her shirt, he was already naked. He looked just as magnificent as she remembered. She let her gaze linger on his taut abdomen, on the finely defined muscles of his thighs and on the mounting evidence of his desire for her.

"Ignore it," he said with a smile. "For now, anyway. You've got some undressing to do."

With great reluctance, Lia averted her gaze. "I—I need to tell you something."

His fingers, which had moved to her shirt front, stilled. He exhaled a breath, watching her closely. "What's the matter?"

"Nothing is the *matter*." Lia felt herself blush. "It's just that m-my body doesn't look the same. I don't want to disappoint—"

"You won't," Shane said with such confidence, Lia believed him. "Now, let's get you out of these dusty clothes."

Shane slipped her shirt off her shoulders. It fell to the

floor and pooled at her feet. The rest of her clothes quickly followed the same path.

She heard his sharply indrawn breath and when she looked up at him, his eyes were unfocused and glazed with desire.

"You're beautiful," he whispered.

Lia lowered her hands, which had risen to cover her nakedness. Mesmerized, she gazed into his eyes and shook her head slowly.

"Yes," he insisted, cupping the back of her head and bringing her mouth to his.

A smoldering heat flared through her, a sensation Lia didn't bother to fight.

His tongue teased the fullness of her lower lip. When she opened her mouth, Shane changed the angle of the kiss, deepening it, kissing her with a slow thoroughness that left her weak and trembling.

"I'll make this good for you." His hands cradled her breasts in his large palms, the nails of his thumbs scraping across the hypersensitive tips.

Lia gasped. A jolt of pleasure sparked between her legs.

His hands remained on her breasts even as his gaze dropped to the soft, round mound of her belly. He planted kisses across her abdomen, murmuring words of endearment. For her? For the baby? Did it matter?

Raw need surged as he continued to kiss and caress her. She was too busy kissing him back to remember stepping into the shower. All she knew was he was soon soaping her down with a large mitt, his talented lips following the rinsing stream of water.

His mouth and hands were all over her body. And everywhere he touched, she sizzled. Caught up in the pleasure swelling like the tide inside her, Lia barely noticed him putting her foot on a small stool before he entered her. His strong arms held her up as the rhythmic thrusts fueled the growing need building inside her. Her muscles tensed and collected. "Don't stop," she groaned, trying to catch her breath.

"Not a chance." His own voice was hoarse with need.

Water rained down as the tension inside her exploded. She rode the rising waves of pleasure, clutching his broad shoulders until the last few twitches left her body, dissolving in a white-hot glow.

Only then did Shane let himself come, shuddering with the force, growling his pleasure against her throat.

This time had been perfect, Lia thought dreamily, resting her head against the hard plane of his chest. Perfect, because of the love.

His hands were gentle as he wrapped her in a warm Turkish towel and efficiently dried her off.

"I tried to go easy," he said earnestly. "I didn't want to hurt the baby."

"You don't have to worry." Lia trailed a finger down his cheek, touched by his concern. "The doctor said as long as I don't go swinging from chandeliers, the baby will be fine. She even said this would be a good time to try different positions."

Without warning Shane scooped her in his arms and carried her into the bedroom, depositing her on the bed with great gentleness.

Lia looked up at him, her pulse rioting. "What are you doing?"

"Just following doctor's orders," he said, a devilish twinkle in his eyes. "We've got a whole lot of positions to try. I figure the sooner we get started, the better."

For the next week Lia and Shane were inseparable. Her days were filled with work, and her evenings and nights, with Shane. He hadn't yet said he loved her, but she saw it in his eyes and felt it in his touch. She clutched tightly the hope that one day they would be a real family.

Though Lia had never been happier, as the baby continued to grow, she found herself increasingly fatigued by the time the workday ended. Making dinner became a chore and many nights she settled for a nap instead of food.

Observing this, Shane put his foot down and insisted she dine with him every evening. Though Lia initially protested, she rather liked being coddled and fussed over. And bit by bit, she began to feel accepted by everyone in his family. Everyone but Sawyer. Although Sawyer was always pleasant on the surface, she got the feeling he was holding back his approval.

"Does Sawyer not like me?" she asked Shane on the drive back to her apartment after an evening concert in the park.

Though he was still pressuring her to move into the ranch house, she'd made it clear that wasn't happening. Of course, rainy nights like this caused her to question that decision.

Shane frowned. "Did he say something to you?"

"No, he's very polite." Lia chose her words carefully, knowing how close the two brothers were and not wanting to start any trouble between them. Besides, she genuinely liked Sawyer.

From the day she'd first started at New Fortunes Ranch, she'd thought he was a great guy. But the comfortable camaraderie they'd enjoyed had disappeared once she'd told Shane she was pregnant. "I feel as if I'm on trial and he's a juror, gathering evidence, trying to make up his mind."

"Sawyer is like that," Shane admitted. "He's cautious. Takes him a while to trust."

Shane could have been describing himself. But since

he'd been suspicious in the beginning then had come to accept she was telling the truth, Lia could only hope that his brother would eventually believe her, too. "I'll win him over."

Shane smiled. "I have no doubt of that."

"I wondered if you'd be interested in going with me to San Antonio on Saturday?" Lia asked. "They're having a big Folklife festival at HemisFair Park. I've attended in the past and it's a lot of fun."

"This weekend isn't good." A long silence passed. "I'll be tied up both days."

This was the first Lia had heard of him being out of town. "Where are you going?"

He pulled the truck to a stop in front of her apartment building. "What do mean where am I going?"

"You said you were going out of town."

"You misunderstood." Shane's voice was well controlled. "We have a guest coming in. Making sure she's entertained will keep me busy all weekend."

There was a tension in his voice that Lia hadn't heard before. "Her?"

"Jeanne Marie." He clamped his lips shut as if he'd already said too much.

"Your old family friend."

His gaze shot to hers.

"Her name came up before," Lia reminded him. "You told me she was an old family friend. Will I get to meet her?"

His answer was immediate and absolute. "No."

Tears stung the backs of Lia's eyes. Darn pregnancy hormones. It wasn't as if she had any interest in meeting some old friend of his parents; she just didn't like feeling shoved to the side.

Okay, and maybe his attitude hurt, just a little.

"Well." Lia forced a smile. "I hope you have a nice weekend with her."

A startled look crossed his face. "You and I will still have tomorrow night."

"I'm afraid not." Lia knew she was being petty but at the moment she didn't care. "*My* old friend from San Antonio may be coming to town. If not, I'll probably spend the evening with Selina. Maybe Dori and Jax will join us."

"Perhaps we could all get together for drinks," he suggested.

"It's a nice thought, but no." She gave him a phony smile. "I'm sure you understand."

Shane rubbed the back of his neck and scowled. His mood showed no signs of improvement on the trek up her apartment stairs. Even the kiss they exchanged at the door was more perfunctory than passionate.

Once inside, Lia called Steph. As expected, it went straight to voice mail but she left a message telling her friend she wanted to set a time to get together. She mentioned she was available tomorrow night, but realized it was short notice... so if that didn't work, another day would be fine.

Then she called Selina and left the same message.

Lia ended the call and plopped back on the bed. The hot, angry tears she'd been holding back began to fall. Tomorrow she might feel better. Tomorrow she might even be more understanding. But right now she couldn't help but wonder if she'd ever fully be a part of Shane's life.

## Chapter Fifteen

Shane had offered more than once to pick up Jeanne Marie at the airport. But she'd insisted on renting a car and meeting them at the ranch.

Wyatt glanced at the clock on the mantel. "She should have been here by now."

Victoria stopped pacing. "She should have been here an hour ago."

"It takes time to pick up a rental car," Shane said.

"How would you know?" Asher gave a little laugh. "You always have a vehicle waiting for you."

Shane resisted the urge to snap at his brother. They were all on edge, knowing this woman held the answers to all their questions, but unsure how those answers would affect their family.

He told himself it was a good thing he hadn't seen Lia last night. The closer it had gotten to Jeanne Marie's visit the more his stress level had risen. Still, not seeing Lia brought its own kind of stress.

He'd grown used to having her in his life. In fact, he couldn't imagine her not being with him. But falling in love so quickly made him uneasy. After a lifetime of guarding his heart, he didn't like feeling vulnerable.

Asher's head jerked up. "Is that a car?"

Shane pushed back the curtains at the parlor window. A large dark sedan pulled to a stop. A tall woman with gray hair stepped out.

*The other woman.* Shane had to turn away. His chest felt as if someone had put it in a vise and was slowly squeezing.

"I'll welcome her at the door," Shane said to his siblings, forcing the words past the tightness in his chest. "Then I'll bring her back here to meet all of you."

The doorbell chimed and Shane was at the door in seconds. Before reaching for the knob, he paused for a moment to take a deep breath and plaster a smile on his face.

He opened the door wide. "Welcome to New Fortunes Ranch, Jeanne Marie."

It wasn't a proper greeting, but Shane couldn't bring himself to call her *Mrs. Fortune.*

He motioned her into the foyer. "I'm Shane. We've spoken so much on the phone, I feel as if I already know you."

"Shane." The older woman's face broadened in a smile. Her arms slipped around him. But before he could react to the unanticipated hug, she released him. "You look so much like your daddy, I swear I'd know you anywhere."

The words were a dagger to his heart.

Thankfully over the years Shane had had a lot of experience keeping his composure and true feelings hidden. Those experiences served him in good stead now.

"I've heard that before." Shane forced a laugh, his smile never leaving his lips. "I'm glad you could make it."

"I appreciate being invited." Her smile was warm, friendly and oddly familiar.

Close-up, Jeanne Marie was a handsome, rather than a pretty, woman. Certainly not the type a man would choose for a mistress or a second wife. She looked to be about his father's age with gray hair pulled back in a low bun and a face with more than a few lines.

Her white pants and blue top with a matching sweater were nice but not sexy in the least. His mother was ten times prettier than this woman, Shane thought.

"Everyone is in the living room," he said smoothly. "They can't wait to meet you."

"I can't believe James has five grown children." Jeanne Marie shook her head, a smile lingering on her lips. "Where do the years go?"

Shane forced himself to keep walking and not respond. From her comments, it appeared as if Jeanne Marie had known his father for a long time. Which meant their affair had not been a recent thing.

"Everyone," Shane said when he entered the living room. "She's arrived."

Introductions went quickly and it wasn't long until Jeanne Marie was settled on the sofa next to Victoria, a cup of coffee in her hand.

"I want to thank you all for giving me such a warm welcome." The older woman glanced around the room. "I wasn't sure how you'd feel, under the circumstances."

Because they'd decided ahead of time that Shane would take the lead in grilling Jeanne Marie for details, all eyes turned to him.

"Well, that's the thing." Shane forced himself to stay seated, despite the almost overpowering urge to pace. "Our father hasn't been exactly forthcoming about any of those circumstances, including how you fit into his life. We hoped you'd be able to give us the details."

A look of dismay crossed Jeanne Marie's face. "I thought for sure James would have told you."

Several heartbeats of silence passed.

"Told us what?" Shane prompted.

"Well," she hesitated, "that I'm his twin sister and—"

Victoria gasped.

"His sister," Asher blurted out, his eyes wide.

"You didn't even know I'm your aunt?" Jeanne Marie looked at Shane.

He slowly shook his head.

"Oh, my stars." Jeanne Marie took a sip of coffee, her hand trembling. "I didn't think that was a secret, too."

"What else don't we know?" Somehow Shane managed to not stumble over the words.

His father's sister. Not his mistress.

She paused and clamped her mouth shut. "I don't think I should say more until I speak with James."

"Why not?" Shane glanced around at his brothers and sister and smiled, hoping to ease the sudden tension in the air. "We're all family."

"Yes, but why didn't your father tell you about me?"

"I don't know," Shane said honestly. "It doesn't make sense."

Although Shane felt relieved to know his father wasn't cheating on his mom, the relief was tinged with anger. His father talked about the importance of family, yet he hadn't even told them he had a twin sister?

If Jeanne Marie was telling the truth, there could be a whole other family of Fortunes out there. More importantly, why hadn't she been in their lives before now?

Several times over the next hour, Shane and his siblings tried in various ways to wheedle more information out of Jeanne Marie. But finding out they knew nothing about her had spooked the woman and she refused to share any other information of substance.

Despite her perceived need to watch her words, Jeanne Marie agreed to stay on for a few days so they could all get better acquainted.

Shane had the sinking feeling that they were going to have to wait until his father returned to the country before they could fully unravel the mystery of Jeanne Marie.

Lia placed her phone on the kitchen counter, feeling oddly melancholy. Perhaps it was the fact that Shane was busy all weekend with an old family friend he didn't want her to meet. Or maybe it was because she'd spent the past ten minutes on the phone laughing and talking with her once best friend, Steph Roberts, wishing they kept in closer touch. Granted, they met twice a year to celebrate birthdays, but was that really enough time to give a woman who'd been her roommate all through college as well as one of her dearest friends?

Then she reminded herself that the distance between them had been deliberate on her part, a self-preservation thing. After living with Steph for a year after graduation, Lia had seen no option but to step away before the fast-paced, extravagant lifestyle began to seem normal. Before she forgot how she was raised and did things she knew she would forever regret.

Making herself a cup of herbal tea, Lia took it with her to the sofa and, with nothing better to do, she let the memories of those days wash over her. If she had to pinpoint where the problems between her and Steph started, she'd have to say with Kimber Delano, a San Antonio society matron and wife of a prominent business owner and city councilman. Because of their friendship with Kimber's daughter, Angie, she and Steph had been invited to par-

ties and cookouts at the Delano mansion in the exclusive
Hill Country Village area.

Shortly before graduation, Kimber had approached
them with a job offer. Lia had been flattered that such a
prominent civic leader would seek her out. Later, she'd
look back and wonder if they'd been sought out not because she and Steph were the prettiest of their group of
friends but because they were the only two who didn't
come from money.

Lia had been impressed with the salary Kimber had
quoted, but curious as to which of Mr. Delano's compa-
nies they'd be working for....

That was when they learned they'd be working for Mrs.
Delano and not her husband. Kimber had explained that
she ran a small, very discreet "matchmaking" service for
highly placed politicians, community leaders and prominent businessmen throughout Texas.

Although she'd couched the duties in all sorts of flow-
ery language, Lia's mother hadn't raised a fool. She remembered how the woman's eyes had narrowed when
she'd blurted out that she'd never be a prostitute. According to Kimber, there was a big difference between what
the women who worked for her did and prostitution.

But Lia couldn't see the difference and immediately
turned down the offer. Steph, on the other hand, had been
intrigued. It wasn't long until her friend began working
for Kimber, embracing the expensive clothes and travel
perks that came with the position. Almost immediately,
Steph was able to afford a luxury condo in Canyon City.

Lia had accepted an entry-level position at a San Antonio accounting firm. For a year, Lia had shared Steph's
condo, paying a tiny fraction of the rent, hoping to convince her friend she deserved better.

But for the pretty blonde girl from the trailer courts,

the money was seductive. Not to mention the chance to rub elbows with the wealthy, attend their parties, even jet off to Paris for a weekend. After a while Lia realized she couldn't change a mind that didn't want to be changed.

They'd parted amicably and tonight they'd set a time and place to celebrate Steph's hitting the quarter-of-a-century mark.

A knock at the door had Lia's head jerking up. A second, louder rap sent her hurrying across the floor, her heart giving a leap. She knew only one person that impatient.

Lia glanced through the peephole. With her hunch confirmed, she slowly opened the door. "Shane. I didn't expect to see you this weekend."

He stepped inside and glanced around. "I hope I'm not interrupting."

"The plans with my friends fell through." She locked the door behind him then turned to him.

After what had happened, she'd told herself she wouldn't be too welcoming when he came around. But the lines of strain around his eyes and the harshness of his features worried her. She couldn't remember seeing him so upset. Except maybe when she'd told him about the baby. Something bad must have happened.

"Did your family friend arrive safely?"

Shane gave a jerky nod, crossed the kitchen and stared out the window, the sound of a police siren seeping through the glass. "I don't like you living here."

Lia crossed the room and stood behind him, placing her arms around his stiff shoulders. "Tell me what you need."

In retrospect, it was probably a silly question. Yet, the words had barely left her lips when he turned, pulled her to him and buried his face in her neck.

"You smell so good." He inhaled deeply. "Like baby powder."

"Supersexy, huh?" she whispered against his dark hair, stroking his arm with the tips of her fingers.

"Works for me." Even before the words left his lips, he was unfastening her gown, pulling it over her head and tossing it on the kitchen table. He backed her up against the wall and began kissing her fiercely. "I need you, Lia."

"Ah, Shane," she said as desire exploded inside her. "I need you, too. But we really have to move this to the bed. Hard floors, tabletops or walls don't work so well for me now."

Without a word, he lifted her effortlessly into his arms and carried her across the room to the Murphy bed already pulled out of the wall.

Lia sensed the pent-up passion humming through him as he deposited her on the bed then lay down beside her. She slipped her fingers under his shirt. "Someone on this bed is overdressed and, for once, it's not me."

The first real smile she'd seen since he arrived tugged at his lips. His clothes soon joined hers on the floor.

There was a desperation to his movements. Whatever had happened today had really upset him.

*And he came to me for comfort.*

Emboldened by the knowledge, Lia reached for him. The lovemaking that followed was fast and furious. She knew his body as well as he knew hers. And if he thought this was all in his hands, she proved him wrong, playing him like a musician played an instrument, drawing him out until they both came together in a crescendo of passion.

Afterward, Shane propped up the pillows and talked. About everything but the family friend who was visiting and what had caused his distress. Lia told herself that eventually Shane would tell her what had upset him.

But before that could happen, she closed her eyes and

felt herself begin to drift off. Her lids flew open when he slipped from the bed and began pulling on his clothes.

"You're leaving?" Her brows pulled together in a frown. "I know my bed isn't as comfortable as yours—"

"I want to stay, but I have…other obligations."

Ah, yes. The mysterious family friend.

His gaze dropped to a piece of paper on the bedside stand. "Are you planning a trip to Boston?"

"My mom wants to come and help me for a few weeks after the baby is born." Lia covered a yawn with her fingers. "We were trying to figure out flights. Are you sure you can't stay tonight?"

She cringed at the hint of a whine in her voice.

"I can't." He sat beside her on the bed, his eyes dark and searching. "I didn't mean to come over here and treat you like some booty call."

Lia tilted her head. "Well, if you had your way with me, I certainly had my way with you, too."

He laughed and pulled her close, kissing her soundly.

"I'll give you a call," he promised.

"See that you do," Lia told him. "Or next time I'm keeping my clothes on."

Even though it wasn't that late by the time Shane returned home, he hadn't expected Sawyer to be downstairs when he walked through the door. But his brother called out and Shane joined him in the living room.

"How did it go with your baby mama?"

Shane shot his brother a hard look. "Her name—as you well know—is Natalia and she sends her regards."

"I'm surprised you came home tonight." Sawyer took a sip of bourbon.

"If you have a problem with Lia and me, just say it."

Sawyer gazed at Shane. "I know what the attorney said, but I'm not convinced you getting so close to her is smart."

The evening's events with Jeanne Marie had left Shane's emotions raw and too close to the surface. Being around Lia had calmed him and planted his feet back on solid ground. She had so much faith in him. When he was with her he felt as if he could handle anything.

Still, he didn't want to discuss Lia with his brother. The depth of his feelings for her went far beyond logic. Shane glanced at the amber-colored liquid in his brother's glass. "Got any more of that?"

Sawyer gestured with his head toward a crystal decanter on a side table.

"Where's Jeanne Marie?"

"Upstairs." Sawyer's lips pursed. "She said she was tired from the flight. Personally, I think it was the shock of finding out Dad had never told us about her."

"There's something more going on that neither of them is telling." Shane poured two fingers of bourbon into a glass. "Why all the secrecy?"

"That's what we've been trying to find out all along," Sawyer said with a snort. "I'm sick of these mysteries."

"Mysteries?" Shane turned and lifted a brow. "I thought we only had one."

"I spoke with Tom. He has another report on Natalia from the private investigator and wants to go through it with us tomorrow."

Shane lifted the glass to his lips but didn't drink. "Us?"

"If she goes after you, it's going to affect the family." Sawyer added more bourbon to his glass. "Plus it'll be good for you to have someone objective there."

Shane tightened his fingers around the glass. "Are you implying, little brother, that I can't be objective?"

"Of course not." Sawyer downed the last of the liquor

in his glass. "I simply think it's good for both of us to hear what he has to say."

Shane shrugged. "Be there if you want."

"Tell me, what's really going on between you two?"

What was going on with him and Lia? A couple of things, really, neither of which his brother would probably be happy to hear. Like, he'd never felt closer to a woman than he did to her. And he loved her. More than he'd ever thought possible.

## Chapter Sixteen

The next day Shane rose early. His goal was to have breakfast with Jeanne Marie and his other siblings before she and Victoria left for a tour of Red Rock and an afternoon of shopping.

Jeanne Marie was as cordial—and as closemouthed—as ever. As he sat across from her at the breakfast table, Shane couldn't shake the feeling he'd met her before.

The attorney was set to arrive at ten o'clock, but Shane got caught up on a long-distance phone call from the Atlanta office and didn't get downstairs until almost ten-thirty.

"Sawyer has been telling me that you and Ms. Serrano have become good friends." Tom took a sip of coffee, a look of approval in his blue eyes. "Smart move."

Shane saw no reason to tell the lawyer that his relationship with Lia had little to do with strategy. "My brother didn't seem to think it was a smart move last night."

"I was concerned it could give her some advantage," Sawyer said.

"The only thing that matters is what the DNA test shows." Tom lifted a peach scone from a dainty china plate and smiled. "Kudos to your cook. These are magnificent."

"Sawyer said you've received a preliminary report from the investigator." The more Shane got to know Lia, the more he believed hiring a P.I. had been a waste of everyone's time and money. He couldn't imagine there were any skeletons in her closet.

"We did." Tom glanced at Shane. "You have more of these delicious scones?"

Sawyer lifted the platter and let Tom choose another one.

"You were saying..." Shane prompted.

"Ah, yes." Tom's gaze grew thoughtful. "Your, er, friend didn't get off to the best start when the father left the household—"

"She told me about that," Shane said.

"She's come a long way and done a fine job building a good life for herself."

Just like Shane thought. *No skeletons.*

"There's only one area that appears to have some possibilities and the investigator is concentrating his efforts there." Tom's lips twisted as though he'd tasted something bitter. "Unfortunately, we're being stonewalled."

Shane set down the coffee cup he'd just raised to his lips, a cold chill traveling through his veins. "What kind of possibilities?"

"Shortly after Ms. Serrano graduated from UT San Antonio, she moved into a very expensive condominium. You may have heard of the Mansions at Canyon Springs?"

Sawyer looked at Shane and he shook his head. "We're not from around here."

"It's a wonderful area, many amenities, but way beyond what a young woman fresh out of college could afford."

Shane thought of the place where Lia currently lived and the one Tom described. "Did she have a lot of roommates? Could that be how she was able to afford the rent?"

"Only one." Tom pulled a file folder from his briefcase. "A Miss Stephanie Roberts. Is the name familiar?"

Shane shook his head. "Could she have been the one paying the rent?"

"Perhaps." Tom shrugged. "But both of them were on the lease."

"How much was rent?" Sawyer asked.

Tom named a figure that made Sawyer whistle.

"Exactly." Tom slid the file into his briefcase and shut it with a snap. "I apologize for how long this is taking. I have my suspicions on what went on, but I prefer not to say until we know for sure. I'll be back in touch."

Tom rose to his feet and Shane and Sawyer followed.

"Thanks for keeping on top of this," Sawyer said.

"If Miss Serrano mentions anything about Stephanie Roberts, be sure and let us know. Any information will be helpful."

"Will do." Shane felt as if he had let Lia down by simply listening to what the attorney had to report.

"I can let myself out." Tom smiled and disappeared down the hall.

"Since you're having lunch with Lia today, that will be a good opportunity for you to bring up college days and her time in San Antonio," Sawyer said.

Shane cocked his head. "What gave you the idea I'm seeing Lia today?"

"She asked this morning if I minded if she took a long lunch. I assumed she was meeting you."

"No, we don't have plans." Shane thought for a moment. "She may be having lunch with Selina or Dori."

"Perhaps she's meeting Stephanie." Sawyer's expression seemed to brighten at the thought.

"C'mon, Sawyer. What would be the odds of that happening?"

His brother shrugged. "Long shots do come in. I won fifty thousand dollars on one just last week."

"That's horses, not people."

"Well, since you're obviously available, why don't you join Nick Lamb and me for lunch? I'm meeting him at the club at twelve-thirty."

Shane thought of all the work he had to do. With his father out of the country, the burden of running JMF Financial had fallen on his shoulders. Because of the Jeanne Marie thing, most of his siblings had already walked away from the company that his father had founded.

But as the COO of JMF Financial, and at one time the man most likely to take over the company when his father retired, Shane found it more difficult to leave the company he loved.

He stood at a crossroads, not sure which direction to take. He'd invested so much of his time and attention into JMF Financial that he wanted to be absolutely sure that leaving was in his best interests. Shane had hoped speaking with Jeanne Marie last night would provide clarity. Unfortunately, that encounter had left him with more questions than answers.

Perhaps having lunch with Sawyer and his friend was what he needed. "Who's this Nick Lamb? Have I met him?"

"I don't think so." Sawyer shrugged. "He's a real-estate developer from San Antonio. A friend of a friend, really. I'm sure he wants to see what he can do for us and what we can do for him."

Shane grimaced. He'd dealt with many such men and already knew what the guy was after—Fortune money to fund some of his more risky projects. "On second thought I'm too busy for lunch."

"You're not too busy." The determined look on Sawyer's face reminded Shane that his brother could be a formidable adversary. "This will be good for you. Trust me. There's nothing like a two-martini lunch to take your mind off woman troubles."

Lia dressed with special care for the birthday lunch with Stephanie. The arabesque-print dress in navy, beige and aqua with a V-neck showed off her increasing décolletage. Navy espadrille wedged sandals made her look taller. She'd slipped on the watchband of stones and beads she'd made the other night, hoping it would draw attention to her slender wrist and away from her belly.

She'd suggested they eat at Red but Steph had insisted on meeting at the Red Rock Country Club. When Lia had told her friend she wasn't a member, Steph had told her not to worry. She had connections.

It appeared, Lia thought with a wry twist to her lips, that nothing had changed.

Because they were meeting at the country club, Lia knew it would be a long lunch. That was why she'd gotten the okay from Sawyer to take additional time.

Lia arrived a few minutes early and parked her car herself. Though using the valet parking would be more convenient, she barely had enough money to pay for both meals and the tip. Her gift to Steph was in her purse: a watchband made out of lapis lazuli stones.

As she stepped onto the curving sidewalk, Lia caught sight of Steph waiting for her at the entrance. Steph's long blond hair, the color of buttermilk, now hung past her shoulders. Her blue linen dress showed off the curves men liked. Though her face was classically beautiful, there was a girl-next-door friendliness to her features that made you want to pull her close rather than take a step back.

Stepping back was actually what Lia had done over two years ago when she'd moved out of the condo they'd shared in Canyon Springs. Yet, seeing her now made Lia remember all over again the good times they'd shared.

"Lia." A genuine smile lifted Steph's shiny pink lips. She opened her arms. "It's been too long."

Steph's voice was melodious and smooth. Even though she was a lifelong Texan, there was only the merest hint of a drawl. She pulled Lia close for a quick hug then held her at arm's length. "The layers in the hair are *très* chic. And that dress is gorgeous. But there's something you didn't tell me…"

Her friend's eyes lowered and Lia could feel herself blushing. Just like she had when she was fifteen and her mother had caught her French-kissing the boy next door.

Lia lifted her chin. "I'm due in September."

"Congrats." Steph linked her arm through hers. "Who's the lucky man?"

"A friend." Lia realized as she said the words they were true. She did think of Shane as a friend. "You don't know him."

"I'm sure I don't, since it's been a while for us." Steph gave a throaty laugh. "But I'm glad you agreed to see me, to keep the birthday lunch tradition going."

There was an odd catch in Stephanie's voice, leaving Lia to wonder if today was about more than keeping that tradition.

Instead of eating inside, they chose a table on the patio. A large green awning, along with discreetly placed fans and misters, kept the area cool and comfortable.

They quickly ordered and the conversation turned to mutual friends from UT and what they were doing now. Surprisingly, Steph had kept in contact with quite a few of the women they'd known in college.

"So—" Steph leaned forward "—tell me about your 'friend.'"

"I will—" Lia took a sip of water "—after you catch me up on what's new with you. You said you're still working for Kimber?"

"I am." Steph toyed with her food. "But just between us, I've grown weary of all the…socializing. And I've met someone…"

"A client?"

"Someone I met at a party. I was there with…a different man."

*A client,* Lia thought to herself, filling in the blank.

"Anyway, Paul and I chatted briefly and really hit it off. I thought I'd never see him again." Steph started talking fast, the way she used to when she was nervous. "Then I ran into him at the grocery store. The connection was still strong and he asked me out."

"Love at first sight." Lia kept her tone light.

"Yes." An adorable blush colored Steph's cheeks. "Does that sound corny?"

Lia thought of Shane. She remembered the attraction that had sparked the instant her eyes had met his. Her lips curved upward and she shook her head. "Not corny at all."

"I've seen Paul several times and…" Steph's expression grew dreamy. She sighed. "Anyway, we're so happy."

"Does he know about your job?"

"No," Steph snapped then immediately gave Lia an apologetic smile. "And he's not going to find out. He's a decent guy, Lia. He wouldn't understand."

"I'm excited for you, Steph." Her friend had a good

heart and Lia wanted nothing more than for her to be happy. "But you can't build a life with this man on a lie."

Steph looked away, but not before Lia saw the sheen of tears in her eyes. "I'm afraid he won't want me if he knows."

Lia reached over and took her friend's hand. "Give him a chance. He might surprise you."

"I don't know—"

"You must tell him." Lia met her friend's troubled gaze. "Texas may be a big state, but it's also a small world. He'll find out eventually. It will be better if it comes from you."

"Hel-lo, ladies."

Steph pulled her hand back at the deep baritone. Even though a friendly smile graced her lips, Lia sensed the sudden tension.

"Nick." Steph gazed up at the man, her welcoming tone giving nothing away. "What a pleasant surprise. I didn't expect to see you in Red Rock."

Nick appeared to be somewhere in his late thirties to early forties. Dark hair. Handsome features that had begun to turn soft from too much good food and drink. The imperious way his assessing gaze swept over Lia told her two things: this man had money and, sometime in the past, he'd been one of Steph's clients.

"I didn't expect to see you here, either." He smiled at Lia. "Aren't you going to introduce me to your friend?"

"Natalia Serrano." Steph pointed to her and then to him. "Nick Lamb."

"What a pretty name. It's a pleasure to meet you, Natalia." He rested his hand on the back of Steph's chair. "Do you and Stephanie work together?"

"I don't want to be rude," Lia said in a cool, dismissive tone she knew Steph couldn't use with a client, "but my friend and I were discussing some important business. So if you don't mi—"

"Nick, I got us a table inside—" Sawyer stopped when he saw Lia. His gaze shifted, taking in the scene before him and lingering on Steph for several seconds before returning to Lia.

"Hi, Sawyer." Though her stomach churned, her voice sounded surprisingly composed.

Nick raised a brow. "You two know each other?"

"Natalia works for me," Sawyer said.

Nick's smile widened.

"She's a CPA," Sawyer added.

"Is that so?" The predatory gleam in Nick's eyes made Lia's skin crawl. "Well, honey, you can work on my... books...anytime."

Sawyer cocked his head. "I didn't realize you and Nick were acquainted."

"We're not acquainted," Lia told him then shifted her gaze to Nick. "And I'm not your honey."

"Actually, it's Steph and I who are old friends," Nick said easily, though his gaze remained on Lia.

Something flared in Sawyer's eyes. "Steph?"

"That's me." Steph held out her hand to Sawyer. "Stephanie Roberts."

He took her hand, a strange look in his eyes. "It's a pleasure to meet you, Miss Roberts."

"Please," she said, "call me Steph."

"I don't think I've seen you around Red Rock, *Steph,*" Sawyer said.

"That's because I live in San Antonio."

Nick smiled at Lia. "Do you live in San Antonio?"

Lia shook her head.

"Perhaps you could come down next weekend." Nick's

gaze focused on the V of her dress. "I'm throwing a big party. Steph knows where I live. You could be my guest."

"That won't be possible."

Lia inhaled sharply. A proprietary hand settled on her shoulder and she swiveled in her seat to find Shane standing behind her.

"Hello, sweetheart." Shane leaned over and brushed a kiss against her cheek.

"Nick, this is my brother Shane," Sawyer said quickly. "He's the COO of JMF Financial."

"Lia and I already have plans for this weekend," Shane continued as if his brother hadn't spoken, his unyielding gaze focused on Nick. "And for every weekend after that."

"I didn't realize—" Nick began.

"Now you know." Shane's blue eyes flashed a warning.

Lia relaxed against the back of her chair and took a sip of water. Once again all was right in her world. Her knight in shining armor would keep lecherous Nick at bay.

"Nice to meet you, Ms. Serrano," Nick said with a polite smile. "Steph, I'll be seeing you…soon."

Steph just smiled and after a few more pleasantries, the men strolled off.

"You've been holding out on me," Steph said as soon as the men were out of earshot. "Tell me all about Mr. Tall, Dark and Delicious."

"Shane is a good friend." Lia's gaze followed him until he disappeared inside the building with Sawyer and Nick. Then she turned back to Steph. "He's also the father of my baby."

## Chapter Seventeen

"Tell me about Natalia," Nick said after their lunch dishes were removed and he'd finished describing several of his current developments. "How did you two meet?"

Nick had a good grasp of business and he'd made some brilliant financial investments. But there was something about him Shane disliked. The way he'd looked at Lia was at the top of that list.

"We met at a party." Shane found himself reluctant to give Nick any more information than necessary. "We've been seeing each other ever since."

He was grateful Lia hadn't stood up, because then he'd be fending off questions about the pregnancy. Then again, maybe that would have been what Nick needed to truly believe she was off-limits. Because she was. To Nick. And to any other man.

"She's a beautiful woman." Nick stroked his chin.

"So is Stephanie," Sawyer interjected.

"I suppose so." Nick waved a dismissive hand. "But there's something almost exotic about those big brown eyes and all that dark hair. Is she open to seeing other men?"

Shane inhaled sharply.

"Nick." Sawyer's laugh sounded strained. "Didn't you hear my brother say that he and Lia have been seeing each other?"

"I heard," Nick said. "But some of the women see more than one man at a time."

Shane could feel the blood draining from his body. "The women?"

"Isn't she an escort?"

"Escort? Why would you think that?" Shane heard the words come from his lips, though he didn't recall saying them.

"Because that's how I know Steph."

"An escort service." Sawyer slanted a sideways glance at Shane on the drive to the ranch. "Odds are that's how Lia was able to afford that high-priced condo in San Antonio."

"She could have simply been living there while her friend paid," Shane said, still trying to make sense of everything he'd heard.

"You don't believe that any more than I do," Sawyer scoffed. "When we walked up to the table I heard Lia tell Nick that she and Steph were discussing business. *Business.*"

"If Lia was an escort, she sure as hell wouldn't be living in the dump by the Red Rock Medical Clinic. And she would have done a better job of protecting herself from getting pregnant."

"Let's assume for a moment that it is your baby. You both took all the precautions and the pregnancy still happened." Sawyer's gaze turned thoughtful. "Maybe she wanted to get out of the…business. When she got pregnant by you, that became her ticket out."

Although what his brother was saying was plausible, Shane started shaking his head even before Sawyer finished speaking. He couldn't believe the Lia he'd come to know, *his* Lia, had ever been a prostitute. "I'm sure there's a logical explanation."

"So you're going to what? Ask her and then believe what she says?"

"Why are you always so willing to think badly of Lia?" Shane frowned. "You hired her. Raved about her. I know you like her."

"You're right," Sawyer admitted. "I do. But you're my brother. And I don't want to see her hurt you. I want you to be smart about this."

Shane raked a hand through his hair. "So what do you suggest?"

"Trust, but verify. Ask her, but in the meantime we give what we know to Tom so he can get it to the investigator," Sawyer suggested, watching him closely. "With this additional information, he should be able to verify whether or not she is, or has ever been, a high-priced escort."

Shane wiped a hand across his face. "I don't like it."

"You don't have to like it." Sawyer gentled his tone. "This is the only way to know the truth. Besides, look on the bright side."

"There's a bright side?"

"If she ever was a prostitute, and that baby turns out to be yours, your chances of gaining full custody just got a helluva lot stronger."

Although doing the ranch payroll kept her busy the rest of the afternoon, the incident at the country club left Lia feeling on edge. She remembered the way Nick's gaze had lingered on her breasts. When she'd complained to Steph that he'd looked at her as if she was a steak and he hadn't eaten in a week, her friend had just laughed and said that was par for the course.

Thankfully Nick hadn't returned to their table, but then neither had Shane. For a few seconds, as Lia watched the printer spit out checks, she worried Shane may have thought she'd *welcomed* Nick's attentions. But she immediately chided herself. Shane knew her better than that…

The end of the day brought a dilemma. Lia wasn't sure if she was welcome at the house tonight for dinner since Jeanne Marie was still around. She'd planned to ask Shane when she saw him.

But he hadn't called. Or stopped by.

Not wanting to intrude on their "family" time, Lia headed straight home. By the time she'd recharged with a thirty-minute power nap and changed into a pair of yoga pants, her spirits had rebounded.

She ate a meal of high-fiber raisin bran, topping it off with a banana that tomorrow would be too ripe. She was just about to pull out her beading supplies when a crisp knock sounded at the door. The rap was quickly followed by another one only a second later.

Lia's lips curved upward. It appeared her impatient Prince Charming had arrived.

She jumped up, swiping her hand through her hair on the way to the door, a bounce in her step.

"Come in." She waved Shane inside. Her smile faded when she saw the look on his face. "What's wrong?"

"How was your lunch?" He crossed the room and took a seat at the table.

"Delicious," she said slowly. "How was yours?"

"Not good." His words were crisp, delivered with military precision.

"I'm surprised." Lia hiked her yoga pants up over her belly and dropped into the chair across from him. "Though I haven't eaten at the country club much, I've never been disappointed. Steph had the tilapia with Parmesan pasta. She said it was fabulous."

Lia knew she was chattering when she went on to describe everything that had been on Steph's plate as well as her own. Still, she couldn't seem to stop herself. There was this bleached anger in the air that she didn't understand.

"Tell me about your friend Stephanie." His tone was the same as ever but the spark of good humor she'd grown used to seeing in his eyes wasn't there.

A feeling of dread washed over her.

*He's simply tired,* she told herself, *and I'm overreacting.*

Shane stared at her, an expectant expression on his face.

"Steph and I were roommates at UT. We were both there on scholarship and always short on money." Lia gave a little laugh. "I think shared poverty brought us closer."

"She looks like she's doing pretty well for herself now," Shane said in a casual tone. "Apparently Nick sees her at parties all the time. Yet, you were the one who caught his eye today."

No, he wasn't simply tired. Clearly something was on his mind.

It had been a long day and Lia was suddenly weary of the cat-and-mouse game he was playing. If he was jealous of Nick, he should just say it. Then she could tell him the truth—that she thought Nick was slimy—and they'd both have a good laugh. "Why don't you just come out and say whatever it is you want to say?"

"Are you aware that Stephanie works as a high-priced escort?"

*Darn that Nick Lamb.* Obviously he couldn't keep his mouth shut. Which was a shame because she'd hoped

Shane would have a chance to form his own first impression of Steph.

She expelled a heavy sigh.

"Lia," Shane said, his tone taking on some urgency. "Did you know that?"

"I did."

"Yet, you're still friends with her."

Lia looked at him quizzically. "None of us are perfect, Shane."

"That's right," he said in an even tone. "Sometimes good people make mistakes. I've always believed someone's past doesn't determine their future."

"Exactly." Lia brightened. This was exactly what she'd wanted Stephanie to understand.

His gaze searched hers. "You lived with her for a year after you got out of college. How were you able to afford such an expensive condo?"

A bad feeling settled around Lia's shoulders like a scratchy wool sweater but she shrugged it off.

"How did you know I lived with Steph?" she asked, suddenly curious. "I never told you."

A muscle in his jaw jumped. "Answer the question, please."

Though Lia sat in the middle of the room, she felt as if her back was pressed tightly against the wall. "You answer mine first."

For a split second, she caught a glimpse of something in his eyes, something that looked an awful lot like guilt.

*Guilt?* What had he done? The hairs on the back of her neck prickled.

"How did you know I once lived with Steph?" Lia asked again.

Shane expelled a harsh breath and raked his fingers through his hair. "Shortly after you approached me with the story about being pregnant with my baby, I hired a private investigator to check into your background."

"The *story* about me being pregnant with your baby?" Lia's voice rose. "It wasn't a story, Shane. It's the truth."

"Yes, yes, I know that..."

Suddenly the rest of what he'd said slammed into her with the force of a Mack truck. "You hired a detective. You didn't trust me."

"I didn't know you."

Perhaps he'd called off the detective, but something in the way he was acting told her the guy was still on the job. "Even after you got to know me, you still kept him working for you."

"Trust, but verify, has always been my motto," he said stiffly, confirming her fears.

She searched his face, looking for some evidence of the man she loved, but came up empty.

"Why, Shane? Why would you do that?" None of this made any sense. "I wasn't asking for money. I told you we could do a DNA test once the baby is born. What possible reason..."

A chill swept over Lia like a driving March rain. Surely not. Surely the man she'd fallen in love with wasn't capable of plotting something so horrific.

"You planned to take the baby from me." A slight crack in his facade told her she'd guessed correctly. "Ohmigod, you were going to take my child."

If it was possible for a heart to shatter, hers was now strewn in a thousand pieces at her feet.

"Lia," he said in that soft, smooth drawl that she had once thought was so sexy. "I didn't know you. We'd only been together that one time and—"

"What about the past month? What about all the time we've spent together since you returned to Red Rock?"

She brushed the tears away and pushed back her chair, too angry to sit. "You could have called off the detective. But you didn't."

He stood and took a step toward her. For a second she thought he might reach out, but his hands remained at his sides.

"I've had…" He paused. "I've had a lot on my mind."

"Ah, yes." She barely recognized the sneering tone as hers. "The mysterious *family business*. That should have been my first clue. You wanted me to share everything about myself but you never reciprocated."

"Well, you were going to take the baby and leave," he blustered.

"What are you talking about?"

"The trip to Boston." His jaw lifted in a stubborn tilt. "You told me you were going to stay, but actually you were planning to leave."

"No, you don't." Lia stepped close and punched him in the chest with a finger. "Don't you dare try to put this on me, mister. Whenever you asked me about anything, I told you the truth. But not you. You wouldn't even tell me why you were so upset over an old family friend being in town."

Shane saw the hurt on her face. He heard the anguish in her voice. But then he remembered how his father had kept a twin sister and another whole part of the Fortune family from him all these years. "Did you ever work as an escort?"

If she had, he just needed to know. He wouldn't use it against her. It was just important he knew she would be honest with him and that he could trust her.

"You know me. You know my heart. How can you ask me such a question?" Confusion and hurt warred with the anger in her eyes. When she pointed to the door, he knew anger had won the battle. "Get out."

"Why won't you answer my question?"

"If you don't know…" She strode to the door and jerked it open. "This conversation is over. If you want to talk with me again, do it through my attorney."

"I didn't think you had a lawyer."

"I'll get one."

"Lia." He placed a hand on her shoulder, overcome with the need to touch her, to reassure himself that she was still his and that they could weather this storm.

She pushed his hand away. "I asked you to leave."

Panic clawed its way up his spine. His world stood on the verge of crumbling beneath his feet and he didn't know how to stop the avalanche. "Lia—"

With a force that surprised him, she shoved him through the open doorway then slammed the door shut.

The dead bolt clicked into place and the last chunk of solid earth beneath his feet gave way.

Instead of immediately heading home, Shane got into his truck and drove. He wasn't sure where he was going; he just knew he didn't want to talk to anyone or think about what had happened.

But it quickly became apparent that no matter how high he turned up the radio, or how fast he drove, all thoughts led back to Lia. While he admitted he could have handled the situation with more finesse, the intensity of her reaction to a simple question had shocked him.

Though he didn't really feel like making conversation and he certainly wasn't hungry, Jeanne Marie and his siblings were expecting him for dinner.

Shane decided he didn't need any more time alone with his thoughts. He needed to be surrounded by his supportive family. For once, he hoped Victoria and Jeanne Marie had lots to say about their shopping trip.

He walked into the house and found the entire family heading toward the dining room.

"Just in time for supper," Sawyer said in a too-hearty tone.

"Is Lia with you?" Sarah-Jane glanced around him, as if hoping the woman would magically appear.

"Who's Lia?" Jeanne Marie asked.

"A friend. She won't be joining us tonight." Shane's tone made it clear the subject was closed.

"Lia is a friend of Shane's who does this marvelous beadwork," Sarah-Jane said as if she hadn't gotten the message that he'd put out there loud and clear. "She makes these watchbands that are so pretty and so unique, well, next time I see her I'm going to ask if she'll make me one."

"I love beadwork," Jeanne Marie said, then launched into a story about one of her friends who'd recently had this perfectly lovely necklace made out of beads.

"What did you find out from her?" Sawyer asked, dropping into step beside Shane, his voice a low whisper.

"I don't want to talk about it."

"That bad?" Sawyer seemed distressed. "I can't say I'm happy with the news. But it will solidify your case against her in the off chance the baby is yours—"

Something inside Shane broke at that moment. "That baby *is* mine," he roared.

The others in front of them turned in one movement.

"What baby?" Jeanne Marie looked intrigued.

Shane resisted the urge to groan.

"Lia, Shane's girlfriend, is pregnant," Sarah-Jane said. When Wyatt shot her a look, she tossed her hair. "Well, she is. It's not like it's a big secret."

"Shane loves her," Marnie said, earning a scowl from Asher, which she promptly ignored. "That's very obvious to everyone."

"This is all very puzzling." Jeanne Marie fixed her gaze on Shane and he thought he saw a hint of censure. "In my day if a man loved a woman, and especially if that woman was carrying his child, they got married."

"It's not that simple, Jeanne Marie." With a hint of admonishment in his tone, Sawyer pulled out her chair.

"I don't see what's so complicated." Jeanne Marie's blue eyes remained focused on Shane.

Eyes so much like his father's, Shane wondered how he hadn't made the connection right away.

"What did you and Victoria do today?" Asher asked his aunt.

"When do you plan to ask this young woman to marry you?" Jeanne Marie asked Shane, ignoring Asher's feeble attempt to engage her in conversation.

"That would be hard to do." Shane took a sip of water, wishing it were something stronger. "Considering she kicked me out of her apartment this evening."

"Oh, my." Jeanne Marie chuckled. "Sounds to me like someone is in the doghouse."

Shane gritted his teeth. Forget supportive family. Being alone on an open roadway was starting to sound better with each passing second.

Sarah-Jane's brows pulled together in worry. "What did you do to make her so angry?"

"Darling." Wyatt covered her hand with his. "Why must you assume this is my brother's fault?"

"No, she's right." Shane expelled a harsh breath. "The, uh, misunderstanding with Lia is totally my fault."

"Totally?" Sawyer asked with a skeptical look.

"Totally." Shane gave a decisive nod. He'd been an ass.

"What are you going to do?" Jeanne Marie leaned forward. "Send her a dozen roses? Serenade her outside her window?"

"After dinner, I'll come up with a plan." Though right now Shane had no idea what that plan would be, he'd come up with something. After all, his future happiness depended on it. "Tomorrow, I'll put that plan into action."

"It'll work." Jeanne Marie stabbed a piece of lettuce with her fork. "Because, like your papa, you're a determined man. And I would hazard a guess, just as stubborn."

Shane's lip quirked upward almost in a snarl.

Jeanne Marie didn't appear to notice. "Once she's speaking with you again, bring your young lady around," she said. "I'd like to meet her. I admire any woman who can stand up to a Fortune."

## Chapter Eighteen

*Come up with a plan,* Shane had said. *Put it into action.*

It sounded so easy when he'd said it. But Shane had quickly discovered figuring out what to do next was more difficult than he'd anticipated.

"All you asked was that she answer one small question," Sawyer reminded him as they stood on the back veranda with a glass of bourbon in hand.

After a long, leisurely dinner, Jeanne Marie had pleaded fatigue and his other siblings and their significant others had left for home. Which left Shane alone with Sawyer.

Shane supposed he could have gone upstairs, but there were still some things he needed to get straight in his head. And Sawyer was always up for playing devil's advocate.

"If she hadn't been an escort, why didn't she simply tell you that?" Sawyer said when Shane didn't answer.

"Because it was an insult for me to even ask. I already knew Lia's moral beliefs would never allow her to go down that road." Shane's eyes remained focused on the night sky. "And if asking wasn't bad enough, she figured out the reason I'd hired the detective was to take the baby from her."

"She had to know you'd never have gone through with that plan." Sawyer put a comforting hand on his shoulder. "Not after you and she had grown so close."

"You mean after I fell in love with her." Shane gave a hollow laugh. "The thing is she doesn't know how much she means to me because I never told her. And I sure as hell didn't show her by my actions today."

While Shane had thought he was being open with Lia—and admittedly he'd let her get a whole lot closer than anyone else he'd ever dated—he'd still held back.

Like when he'd kept her in the dark about Jeanne Marie. Or when she'd asked him to go with her to her last doctor's appointment. He'd refused even though he'd wanted to go. Why? Because he was afraid. Afraid of getting too close. Afraid of caring too much and being hurt.

Yet Lia had opened her heart and arms to him. He'd taken all her love. Then had the audacity to ask if she'd ever been a whore.

He swore.

"I think you're being too hard on yourself. All you did was ask if she'd ever worked for an escort service. It wasn't like you were accusing her of anything."

"Don't you understand, Sawyer?" Shane could hear the tension in his voice. "I know Lia. Because she let me get to know her. No artifice. No posturing. She's the real deal. It was wrong for me to ask. And I should have called off that detective weeks ago."

"We've both been fooled before," Sawyer reminded him.

"That's what led me to this point. You get burned a few times and believing in someone becomes difficult." Shane raked a hand through his hair. "My God, we didn't even trust our own father. We'd convinced ourselves that he had a whole other family stashed somewhere."

"Hey, we asked numerous times for an explanation and he always shut us down. Then he goes and gives sixty percent of the stock in our family company to some mysterious woman." Sawyer began pacing the veranda. "That would make anyone suspicious."

"But we jumped to a whole bunch of very damning conclusions before we had all the facts." Shane pinned his brother with his gaze. "We actually thought Dad had another family—that he'd been cheating on our mother. This is a man we've known our whole lives. What does that say about us?"

"He was acting suspicious." Sawyer refused to give any ground. "And giving away all that stock with no explanation? Crazy."

"You're absolutely correct," Shane said. "And I agree he has some explaining to do. But there was something Lia said to me that I can't get out of my head."

Shane paused. He knew it sounded girlie, but it struck at the heart of where he'd gone wrong with her, and where he'd gone wrong with his father.

"What did she say?" Sawyer prompted.

"That when you know someone's heart, you know what they're capable of doing." Shane expelled a harsh breath. "I know Lia. She isn't capable of being an escort or of lying to me about the baby's paternity."

"You're certain."

Shane nodded.

"Then go to her," Sawyer said in a matter-of-fact tone. "Apologize. Tell her you were an ass and then you two can move on."

*If only,* Shane thought, *it could be that simple.*

\* \* \*

Lia glanced down at her clean desk with a sense of satisfaction. Last night, in a weak moment, she'd considered calling in sick. She'd even toyed with the idea of quitting. But her mother had instilled in her too strong of a work ethic for either choice to be an option.

Besides, not only did she need the money, taking care of payroll yesterday had left her behind on her other duties. Yet as busy as she'd been all day, she never stopped worrying that Sawyer or Shane might stop by. But it was almost time to leave for the day and she hadn't seen either one.

Perhaps continuing to work here until the regular bookkeeper returned wouldn't be a problem after all. But when the bells over the door jingled at four fifty-five and she saw Sawyer in the doorway, she realized she'd been too optimistic.

A knot formed in the pit of her stomach. She had no doubt her boss knew all about her conversation with Shane. He'd either come to admonish her, fire her…or both.

"Do you have a few minutes to talk?" he asked in a courteous tone.

Dressed casually in jeans, a chambray shirt and cowboy boots, he reminded her of the nice man who'd hired her all those weeks ago.

"Of course," she said in a businesslike tone. He was, after all, her employer. "What's on your mind?"

Lia hoped he'd just blurt out whatever he'd come to say. Instead he moved the tax guides from the chair next to her desk and took a seat.

He cleared his throat. "It's rather warm out there today."

"I heard on the radio it hit ninety, which normally we don't see until late June." Lia heard herself say the words, unable to believe she was having a conversation with Sawyer about the *weather*.

"I owe you an apology."

For a second she wasn't sure she'd heard correctly. "What did you say?"

The shape of his mouth and his blue eyes reminded her so much of his brother. The man who'd plotted to take her child from her.

"I know Shane shared with you some experiences he's had in the past with scheming women. I've had similar encounters." His gaze searched hers. "I'm afraid those past incidents caused me to doubt the veracity of your claim against my brother. I urged him to make sure he looked out for himself."

Before Lia could respond, Sawyer rested his hand on her forearm. "But Shane has convinced me the baby is his. I'm truly sorry for doubting you and I'd like it if we could get back to our old footing and be friends."

His gentle touch was nearly her undoing. But then she recalled Shane's plans to take her baby. Had Sawyer been part of that effort?

Lia lifted her chin. "Did you know your brother hired an attorney *and* a detective to get dirt on me so that he could take my baby?"

Wincing, Sawyer sat back in his chair. "Actually, bringing those two into the picture was my idea."

She started to sputter, but he held up a hand. "On the off chance the baby was a Fortune, it seemed prudent to make sure Shane would have the opportunity to raise his child."

"I understand him having some concerns at first, but after he got to know me…"

"I can't speak to that—" Sawyer began but stopped when the bells over the door jingled and Shane walked in.

For a second Lia wondered if this was some sort of planned tag-team effort, but Sawyer appeared startled to see Shane.

"Is this a private party or is anyone invited?" There were dark shadows under Shane's eyes and lines of fatigue bracketed his lips. His smile appeared strained.

"The party is over." Lia pushed back her chair and awkwardly rose to her feet. She turned to Sawyer. "I appreciate your honesty. It's a refreshing change."

Sawyer glanced at his brother's rapidly darkening expression before turning back to Lia. "If there's anything I can do to help, please let me know."

"There is one thing." Lia kept her eyes off Shane and firmly on Sawyer. "Walk me to my car."

"She wouldn't even talk with me," Shane fumed, watching the taillights of Lia's car disappear into the distance. "And you, you walked her to the car like some goddamn bodyguard."

"We just mended our fences, so to speak," Sawyer said, not sounding apologetic at all. "How could I refuse?"

"You could have said, 'No, Lia, you need to stay and talk with my brother.'" Shane shoved his hands into his pockets and scowled. "How can we make up if she won't talk to me?"

Sawyer stroked his chin, his gaze turning thoughtful. "It appears to me that some kind of grand gesture is necessary."

If his brother was thinking of flowers or candy or spending a boatload of money on her, Shane knew those gestures would never work. Lia had decided she couldn't trust him. Which didn't bode well for him having a life with her or the baby in the future.

Shane set his jaw. "Call the attorney and tell him I want him out here by seven."

"Do I look like your secretary?" Sawyer responded with a heavy dose of sarcasm.

Shane gave him the big-brother stare that had worked since they were boys. "Call him, Sawyer."

"Okay, okay. Don't get your shorts in a wad." Sawyer pulled out his phone and punched in some numbers. "Tom's going to ask why you want to see him."

"Just get him out here." Shane clenched his jaw tight. In a crisis a man needed to be decisive. He hoped Lia would understand that he'd simply run out of options.

The rest of the week passed quickly with no further visits from Shane, either at work or at home. Oddly, being angry and disappointed didn't stop Lia from missing him. While she may not have seen Shane, Sawyer had been very solicitous, bringing her nutritious midday snacks and ice-cold bottles of water.

She couldn't help feeling glad their friendship was back on track. He seemed happy about it, too. When she asked him for Friday afternoon off for a doctor's appointment in San Antonio, he told her to take the whole day.

As Lia sipped the ice water and nibbled on the gourmet wafers and cheese in a small bistro not far from the large medical plaza, she tried to tell herself it was no big deal to go to her appointment alone. After all, she'd gone by herself to all the previous ones.

The only difference was, when she'd made the appointment for the 3-D ultrasound with Dr. Gray, Lia had envisioned Shane at her side, oohing and aahing over the images of their growing baby.

"Would you like something else besides the herb crisps and Brie, miss?" the perky young waitress asked. Lia blushed, wondering if the waitress had heard her stomach growl. "No, thank you."

The nurse at the office had told her to bring something

sweet to drink during the exam, but to steer clear of sweet foods and drinks for an hour prior to the appointment.

Lia glanced at her watch and grimaced. She still had twenty minutes to kill until her appointment. She took a sip of water just as her phone rang.

Seeing the name on the screen, Lia answered immediately, grateful for the distraction. "Hi, Steph. How's your day going?"

"I've got the most exciting news." Her friend's voice shook with excitement.

"You and Paul?"

"Ah, no." There was hesitation in the bubbly voice now. "This guy is an Italian, big in the oil industry. He's in the States for three weeks and there'll be all sorts of parties—"

"He's a client."

"He's a very important man who needs someone to attend parties with him and—"

"Sleep with him."

"I thought you'd be happy for me."

"I was happy when I heard about Paul," Lia said slowly. "Have you talked with him?"

"You mean did I tell him how I make my living?" Steph gave a little laugh. "No, because I decided it wouldn't have worked out anyway. I like fancy parties and flying in private jets. I was crazy to think I could give it up."

Lia knew the choices her friend made weren't really any of her business, but the last time they'd seen each other, Steph had seemed sincere about wanting to start a new life. "Don't you want more?"

"I can't believe you're asking me that. Like your life is so appealing." Steph snorted, her tone turning derisive. "Living in a dumpy apartment, buying last season's clothes at consignment shops and convincing yourself you're in style. Oh, and I forgot, being pregnant and alone. Yeah, that's what I want."

Several tears slipped down Lia's face before she could stop them. Put that way, her life did sound pretty pathetic. She blotted her eyes with the napkin retrieved from her lap.

For several heartbeats there was silence at the other end of the line.

"I'm sorry, Lia," Steph said softly. "That was just plain mean. I guess I hoped you'd be happy for me."

"I want you to be happy" was the best Lia could manage.

Some of the excitement returned to Steph's voice. "This is really a fabulous opportunity. I'll call you once the assignment is over."

As the call disconnected, a wave of sadness washed over Lia. She remembered so vividly those two young girls with pie-in-the-sky hopes and dreams. Now it looked as though Steph was too scared to let go of the perks of a fast-paced lifestyle to pursue true love. And Lia, well, her true love had hired a detective to take her baby from her.

Lia motioned for the waitress to bring another order of cheese and crackers. The additional plate had just been delivered when Shane walked in the door. Lia's traitorous heart flip-flopped. It was understandable given the circumstances. He looked good enough to eat in a hand-tailored black suit, crisp white shirt and black oxfords.

She knew the instant he spotted her. He crossed the room in several long strides, pulled out a chair and sat down. "Mind if I join you?"

"As a matter of fact, I do." Lia scowled, wishing she wasn't so glad to see him. "Until the baby is born and the DNA test is completed, I have nothing to say to you. If you have questions, you can talk with my attorney."

"Do you have an attorney, Lia?" he asked gently.

"I hired one yesterday." She saw no need to tell him that her new attorney didn't have a fancy office with an impressive address. Or that he worked for legal aid doing pro bono work.

"Good," Shane said, surprising her. "Then you can have him look at this."

He pulled a document out of his coat pocket and handed her several sheets of official-looking paper.

Her stomach churned at the sight of the documents. For a second she thought she might be sick. She took several shallow breaths until the nausea passed. She didn't need to read them to know what they said. He wanted her to relinquish custody.

Lia took a noisy sip of water, the glass unsteady in her shaking hand. Slowly and carefully she placed it back on the table. Somehow she needed to make him understand the mistake he was making. "A baby needs its mother, Shane. I know you can hire a nanny or a nurse, but it won't be the same. And no employee will love this child the way—"

His hand unexpectedly closed over hers. He gave it a squeeze. "Read the document, Lia."

The warmth of his touch was nearly her undoing, but she slipped her fingers from his and focused on the paper before her. She read silently, widening her eyes as the words sank in. When she'd finished, she looked up in disbelief.

"You're waiving your right to custody." As happy as she was to read those words, her heart twisted. "You don't want the baby after all. Was all this just a game to you?"

He raked a hand through his hair. "I worried that's what you'd think."

"What else am I supposed to think?"

"First, I absolutely want to be a part of our child's life."

The fervor in his tone took her by surprise. "But I needed you to know that I have no intention of taking our baby from you. This was the only way I could think to make that clear."

She glanced at the paper. "It looks legal."

"It is." Shane smiled and for a second she found herself smiling back. "Have your attorney check it out."

Lia didn't know what to think. The feelings of relief welling up inside her made it difficult for her brain to process everything that had happened in the past ten minutes. Beginning with him showing up at this out-of-the-way bistro.

"How did you know I was here?" she asked right before the answer slapped her up the side of the head. "Oh, that's right. The *detective*."

She grimaced, the word bitter on her tongue.

"I'm sorry about that, Lia." His blue eyes were serious and intense. "I should have called him off long ago. And I did. That same night you and I last talked."

"If the detective is off the payroll, how did you find me?"

"GPS." He glanced at the table. "You're using a company phone."

"Have you had a chance to look at the menu, sir?" the waitress said in a cheery tone as she strolled up.

Shane smiled. "Just coffee. Black."

Once the waitress had left, Shane's eyes turned thoughtful. "You looked upset when I walked up."

"I was talking to Steph." Disappointment clogged Lia's throat. "She was telling me about her latest…assignment."

"Oh" was all he said.

"Don't you want to ask if I've ever taken those kind of assignments? No?" she said to his continued silence. "You were certainly interested in the answer to that question the other night. You kept asking and ask—"

"Lia," Shane said softly. "I know the answer."

She lifted her head. "What if I told you I'd once worked as an escort?"

"If that were true, I'd say both of our pasts are littered with things we look back on with regret." He squeezed her hand again. "But it's a moot point because your moral character wouldn't allow you to go down that road."

"I slept with you the same night I met you."

Shane flashed a smile. "That's because I'm irresistible."

Lia chuckled and the tightness in her chest began to ease.

"Seriously," he said. "I should have never asked that question. It was an insult."

Her lips lifted in a sly smile. "I'm sure my performance in bed would have been a whole lot better if I had been an escort."

"You were perfect. No complaints from me." Shane released her hand and sat back as the waitress reappeared with his coffee.

"Anything else I can get you?" she asked.

"We're good," Shane said then refocused his gaze on Lia once the waitress sauntered off. "I love you, Lia. I want both you and the baby in my life."

Lia took a bite of the wafer. Oh, how she wanted to believe him. "You hired an investigator to dig up dirt on me."

"At the time it seemed the prudent thing to do. You weren't the first woman to make such a claim. I was angry, Lia, and in shock. And…disappointed. I'd already started falling for you."

"Even if that was true, after we started seeing each other, you didn't call him off."

"Honestly, I didn't think much about him," Shane said. "I knew he wouldn't find anything."

"You didn't trust me. You—"

"I did trust you."

"No." She shook her head from side to side. "If you would have trusted me, you wouldn't have kept secrets from me about the important things going on in your life."

"Ah," he said. "Jeanne Marie."

"Her coming here was important to you." Lia's voice shook with emotion. "Yet, you shut me out. You're still shutting me out. That's why it's difficult for me to believe you when you say you love me."

"You're right. I owe you the truth. A year ago, I never knew Jeanne Marie Fortune existed." Shane's eyes took on a faraway look and he went on to tell Lia the whole story. About how secretive his father had been. How they'd discovered the woman had been going by the last name Fortune. And how they'd feared their dad had a whole other family.

"Until she got here, none of us even knew my father had any siblings other than his brother, John Michael," Shane concluded. "It's so intensely private and I'm not used to sharing family stuff, but I know I can trust your discretion."

"Oh, Shane, I can't imagine what that must have been like, wondering if your father was a bigamist."

"I was wrong there, too. That shouldn't have been one of the first things I thought of as a possibility." Shane cleared his throat, looking both uncomfortable and contrite. "My father is an honorable man."

"You know his heart."

Shane nodded. "I know yours, too, Lia. And I want it to belong to me."

"Oh, Shane," she said, smiling through her tears. "It already does."

## *Epilogue*

"I think this would be a good room for the nursery." Shane spread the blueprint out on Sawyer's dining room table. He'd just picked up the rendering of the house they would build on ranch land outside of Red Rock from the architect that morning.

Lia agreed with Shane that this small Texas town would be a good place for their child to grow up.

"We could paint the walls pale blue," Lia said dreamily. "It's a soothing color."

"And perfect for a boy," Shane said, with obvious pride.

The girl that they had thought they'd be having had quickly changed into a boy when the 3-D ultrasound had captured a good frontal view. Since that appointment Shane had attended every doctor's visit with Lia. And he planned to be in the delivery room when their son was born.

"I wonder if your parents will be back in time for the birth."

"No idea." Shane's lips pressed together. "Everyone in the family is cutting their ties with JMF Financial. I don't want to abandon ship until I know why my father did what he did and where Jeanne Marie figures in all of this."

"It will become clearer with time." Lia slipped her arm through his. "You're doing the right thing in waiting. Once you have the whole story, you can make your decision."

"Speaking of decisions—" Shane turned to her "—I have a question for you."

Lia knew immediately what it was. After all, he'd been asking her to move in with him every day. "And I bet I know what it is."

"Perhaps," he said with a mysterious smile. He took her hand in his and they walked to a bench on the veranda. Even after they were seated, he kept her hand firmly locked in his. "I hope I've shown you that I'll be a good father to our baby."

Lia leaned forward and kissed him on the lips. "You'll be a fabulous daddy."

"I also want to be a fabulous husband." He dropped to one knee in front of her and in that moment everything around her switched to slow motion. "I love you, Lia. More than I ever thought it possible to love a woman."

Her eyes grew large. Though he'd taken every opportunity to tell her how much he loved her, there was a promise in those azure eyes today that she hadn't seen before.

Shane pushed a strand of dark hair back from her cheeks with gentle fingers. "You're strong and intelligent and creative. You're a caring person who brightens my days just by being a part of it. I can't imagine life without you."

He reached into his pocket and pulled out a tiny black velvet box. When he flipped it open, Lia gasped at the large marquise-cut diamond.

"Natalia Serrano, I love you with my whole heart. I would be honored and proud if you would be my wife."

"Well, Shane Fortune, it just so happens that I love you with my whole heart and—" Emotion clogged her throat, making it impossible to continue.

"And—" Shane prompted.

"And yes," Lia sputtered. "Yes, I'll marry you."

"Soon," he said. "Perhaps there's still time to change the double to a triple wedding."

She wondered if he realized Asher and Wyatt and their fiancées, whom she already thought of as friends, were getting married in two weeks. Still, she couldn't think of anything better than sharing a wedding day with them. "I've always dreamed of a June wedding."

He slid the ring onto her finger and suddenly she found herself in his arms. They kissed until they were breathless and laughing. Then they kissed some more…until the baby kicked her hard, as if saying, *Don't forget about me. Mi amorcito.*

Lia's hand dropped to her growing belly and she thanked God that her child—*their* child—would be born into the large, loving Fortune family. With two parents who not only loved him…but each other, as well.

\* \* \* \* \*

*Don't miss the next installment in the new
Special Edition continuity*
THE FORTUNES OF TEXAS:
SOUTHERN INVASION

*Free-spirited Sawyer Fortune and fiercely
independent pilot Laurel Redmond seem like a good
pairing. But their determination to keep things casual
backfires when Mr. I Don't suddenly decides
he wants a bride!*

*Look for*
*A CHANGE OF FORTUNE*
*by Crystal Green.*
*On sale June 2013,*
*wherever Harlequin books are sold.*

# SPECIAL EDITION

**Life, Love and Family**

Be sure to check out the last book in this year's
THE FORTUNES OF TEXAS:
SOUTHERN INVASION
miniseries by Crystal Green.

Free-spirited Sawyer and fiercely independent
Laurel seem like two peas in a pod. But their
determination to keep things casual backfires when
Mr. I Don't suddenly decides he wants a bride!

**Look for *A CHANGE OF FORTUNE* next month
from Harlequin® Special Edition®.
Available wherever books and ebooks are sold!**

HSE65745

# REQUEST YOUR FREE BOOKS!
## 2 FREE NOVELS PLUS 2 FREE GIFTS!

**♦ HARLEQUIN®**

# SPECIAL EDITION
## Life, Love & Family

---

**YES!** Please send me 2 FREE Harlequin® Special Edition novels and my 2 FREE gifts (gifts are worth about $10). After receiving them, if I don't wish to receive any more books, I can return the shipping statement marked "cancel." If I don't cancel, I will receive 6 brand-new novels every month and be billed just $4.74 per book in the U.S. or $5.24 per book in Canada. That's a savings of at least 14% off the cover price! It's quite a bargain! Shipping and handling is just 50¢ per book in the U.S. and 75¢ per book in Canada.* I understand that accepting the 2 free books and gifts places me under no obligation to buy anything. I can always return a shipment and cancel at any time. Even if I never buy another book, the two free books and gifts are mine to keep forever.

235/335 HDN F45Y

Name _____ (PLEASE PRINT)

Address _____ Apt. #

City _____ State/Prov. _____ Zip/Postal Code

Signature (if under 18, a parent or guardian must sign)

### Mail to the **Harlequin® Reader Service:**
**IN U.S.A.:** P.O. Box 1867, Buffalo, NY 14240-1867
**IN CANADA:** P.O. Box 609, Fort Erie, Ontario L2A 5X3

**Want to try two free books from another line?**
**Call 1-800-873-8635 or visit www.ReaderService.com.**

* Terms and prices subject to change without notice. Prices do not include applicable taxes. Sales tax applicable in N.Y. Canadian residents will be charged applicable taxes. Offer not valid in Quebec. This offer is limited to one order per household. Not valid for current subscribers to Harlequin Special Edition books. All orders subject to credit approval. Credit or debit balances in a customer's account(s) may be offset by any other outstanding balance owed by or to the customer. Please allow 4 to 6 weeks for delivery. Offer available while quantities last.

**Your Privacy**—The Harlequin® Reader Service is committed to protecting your privacy. Our Privacy Policy is available online at www.ReaderService.com or upon request from the Harlequin Reader Service.

We make a portion of our mailing list available to reputable third parties that offer products we believe may interest you. If you prefer that we not exchange your name with third parties, or if you wish to clarify or modify your communication preferences, please visit us at www.ReaderService.com/consumerchoice or write to us at Harlequin Reader Service Preference Service, P.O. Box 9062, Buffalo, NY 14269. Include your complete name and address.

HSE13R

"Do you have a long-range business plan?"

She laughed softly. "I love this place. I'll do anything to keep it."

"There's no sense driving yourself to an early grave over a piece of land, Annie."

"Spoken like a vagabond. Well, I've been a vagabond. Roots are so much better." She shoved away from the railing. "I have work to do."

Annie went inside, her good mood having fizzled. What did he know about the need to own, to succeed? He didn't have a child to support and raise right. Who was he to give such advice?

Mitch hadn't come in by the time Austin went to bed and she'd showered and retreated to her own room. It wasn't even dark yet. She pulled down her shades, blocking the dusky sky. Usually she dropped off almost the instant her head hit the pillow.

Tonight she listened for sounds of him, the stranger she was trusting to treat her and her son right. After a while, she heard him come in, then the click of the front door lock.

A few minutes later the shower came on. She pictured him shampooing his hair, which curled down his neck a little, inviting fingers to twine it gently.

Some time passed after the water turned off. Was he shaving? Yes. She could hear the tap of his razor against the sink edge. If they were a couple, he would be coming to bed clean and smooth shaven....

The bathroom door opened and closed, followed by his bedroom door. After that there was only the quiet of a country night, marked occasionally by an animal rustling beyond her open window. She'd finally stopped jumping at strange noises, had stopped getting up to look out her window, wondering what was there. She could identify most of the sounds now.

And tonight she would sleep even better, knowing a strong man was next door. She could give up her fears for a while, get a solid night's sleep and face the new day not alone, not putting on a show of being okay and in control for Austin.

Now if she could just do something about her suddenly-come-to-life libido, all would be right in her world.

\*\*\*

*Don't miss* **A COWBOY'S RETURN** *by USA TODAY bestselling author Susan Crosby.*

*Available June 2013 from Harlequin® Special Edition® wherever books are sold.*

# SPECIAL EDITION

### Life, Love and Family

Coming up next month from *USA TODAY*
bestselling author Marie Ferrarella…

## WISH UPON A MATCHMAKER

A precocious four-year-old sets out to enlist the
help of "the lady who finds mommies" for her
widower father. But there's one obstacle the
matchmaker must overcome to help him realize
true love.

*Look for Ginny and Stone's story in June from
Harlequin® Special Edition® wherever books are sold.*

HSE657469

# HARLEQUIN®

*A Romance FOR EVERY MOOD™*

# Love the Harlequin book you just read?

### Your opinion matters.

Review this book on your favorite book site, review site, blog or your own social media properties and share your opinion with other readers!

Look next month for a very
special **BONUS** story in all four
Harlequin KISS
books!

## THE WEDDING DRESS DIARIES

by Aimee Carson

---

**This story is the exciting prequel to
The Wedding Season collection kicking off in July:**

*Four friends. Three weddings. Two explosive secrets.
One unforgettable summer!*

**Look for this BONUS story across all June
Harlequin KISS books.**

**Available May 21, 2013!**

www.Harlequin.com

ISBN-13:978-0-373-65740-7

SPECIAL EDITION

Life, Love & Family

# JUST A KISS AT NEW YEAR'S

That was all Natalia Serrano had intended. She couldn't believe she had slept with a complete stranger! Lia had never done anything so out of character in her life. Now, against all odds, she was pregnant—and she had no idea how to find her mysterious, memorable lover.

It had been months since Shane Fortune had been in Red Rock. But no amount of time could have prepared him for the revelation that Lia was expecting. *His* child, she said. The distrustful Fortune executive vowed to take control of the situation. What he couldn't control, however, was the hold the beautiful Latina and her unborn baby were quickly taking over his heart....

THE FORTUNES OF TEXAS: SOUTHER[N]

A little taste of Southern Fortune!

$5.50 U.S./$6.25 CAN.

ISBN-13: 978-0-373-65740-7

50550

9 780373 657407

EAN

CATEGORY
HOME AND FAMILY

HARLEQUIN® SPECIAL EDITION

harlequin.com